Things Every Good Woman Should Know

Volume 2

Dear God, Did My Boaz Get Hit by a Bus?

Jae Henderson

Things Every Good Woman Should Know, Volume 2: Dear God, Did My Boaz Get Hit by a Bus?

Printed in the United States
Put It In Writing
274 North Parkway
Memphis, TN 38105

Thank you to all the men who helped me learn to value myself.

FOREWORD

Many women of Christian faith have begun referring to the perfect man as "Boaz." Boaz, the kinsman redeemer, is found in the Bible in the book of Ruth. It contains a beautiful love story indeed, but I don't think women are doing themselves any justice by comparing him to men of today. Yes, he has several admirable attributes that we can all appreciate, but when I describe my future husband, I personally prefer the term "Mr. Righteous." He's Mr. Right, but he loves the Lord and acts like it. He pays his tithes, is active in church, never misses the opportunity to give an encouraging word, and uses his talents to further his career and the kingdom. Yes, he is attractive, but he only has to be attractive to me, since I am ultimately the one who has to wake up to him every morning. He also has money. That is because he understands that faith without works is dead, and he works his behind off to be able to provide for himself and the people he loves. Yet, I have one question, Lord . . . When the heck is he gonna get here? Was he hit by a bus?

No matter whether we call him Boaz or Mr. Righteous, there are plenty of women asking the same question. I don't have an answer for myself or you, but what I do have are some great—and not so great—stories about what I and others have gone through while he rides his bike to get to me. Yes, he must be on a bicycle or on foot or swimming across the ocean because if he wasn't, he would be here already. Lord, please put him on a jet . . . please, please, please.

Within this book you will find a selection of short stories I created to help single women stay encouraged. It's also important that we examine ourselves to make sure we are being the type of woman someone would want to be in a relationship with. Please feel free to laugh, cry, and love with these characters who have found themselves in some interesting situations. Some of them you may find familiar.

I have no idea when my Mr. Righteous will arrive. You probably don't know when yours will arrive either, but I refuse to sit around and be miserable simply because I'm single. I plan to enjoy single life to the fullest and praise my Lord for what He's already done and what He's going to do. Because no matter what happens, I'm going to be all right. Can I get an amen?

TABLE OF CONTENTS

Does Boaz Still Exist?

Wait patiently for the LORD. Be brave and courageous. Yes, wait patiently for the LORD.— Psalms 27:13

Rachel "Waiting-on-my-Boaz" Hill smiled when she realized that she had received another message from Tyler. She and Tyler had recently begun dating, and he often used his phone to let her know she was on his mind. After opening its contents, her eyes grew as big as baseballs, and she quickly flipped over her phone. Rachel was at work and did not want one of her supervisors to walk up behind her while she was staring at a picture of a man's erect penis. It was followed by the text:

PUT ON SOME PRETTY PANTIES AND HEELS AND TAKE A PIC FOR ME. #TOPLESS

It was an impressive penis as far as penises go, but she wondered what in the world would compel a man she had only known two weeks to do that. Sex was the furthest thing from her mind. Well, maybe not the *furthest*, but his sexual gesture was not welcomed. Then he had the nerve to ask her to send a seminude photo. She was a single mother to a preteen girl and had to set an example. She was always telling Felicity and her friends to be mindful of the pictures they sent on their cell phones. Sexting was *not* okay in her home. Who knows where those pictures could end up? What if she decided to run for a political office one day? Those pictures could be used to ruin her.

Tyler seemed like such a nice, respectful man. Rachel headed toward the bathroom and before she reached the door, she was dialing the number of the sender.

"Hey, Sexy." Any other day, the bass from that clearly masculine voice would have made her swoon, but this day, at this moment, it was irritating.

"How dare you!" she hissed.

"What do you mean?" said Tyler.

"How dare you send me a picture of your penis and then ask me to reciprocate like I'm some common chick on the street. I am the woman you wife—*not* the woman you one-night, but evidently you are too busy thinking with the head between your legs instead of the one between your ears. We are Facebook friends. Didn't you see the 'Waiting-on-my-Boaz' in my profile name? That should have told you that I was a woman of God."

"I don't see what you're so upset about," laughed Tyler. "I thought you would like it. As for the picture I want you to send me, if you are scared someone might see it, cut the head off."

His laughter only irritated Rachel more. "Why should I do that? Because I like you? Does that make you think I want to see you naked or I want you to see me naked? You are sorely mistaken. The only thing I wanted you to disrobe was your mind and your emotions. We just met. It is too soon for you to be insinuating something sexual would take place between us. I don't even know you. Just cut the head off! That's all I am to you, isn't it? A body—tits, tail, and hips!"

"Rachel, I'm sorry. I thought you would like it. Other women enjoy my penis pics and showing off their body. I thought you would too. I bet you look great in lingerie. That picture is my way of showing you what you could have if things go well between us."

"You just killed any chance of that happening, you pervert. I'm not like other women, and I have no desire to be a part of your team of women who titillate you and enjoy getting your penis pics. You, sir, are not the man I thought you were. Because a gentleman would know you don't send that type of picture to a lady. We've only been on one date. Lose my number, loser!!!"

"It's your loss. Well, Ms. Waiting-On-My-Boaz, your name isn't Ruth, and I suggest you let go of such antiquated notions of dating. You better stop waiting and jump onboard before you get left like the people who didn't get on Noah's ark. There's a reason you're still single without even a sliver of a man to hold on to at night. You're going to go drown in a self-inflicted pool of loneliness."

"You're right, my name isn't Ruth. It's Rachel, and my mother's name isn't Naomi. It's Earline, and if I were to tell her how you were disrespecting her baby girl, she would ask me for your address and show up on your doorstep with either her belt or her shotgun to teach you some manners. Get off my phone, fool, and lose my number, loser!"

Rachel didn't wait for a response this time. She hit the end button on her phone and laid it on the counter in front of her. She took a long, hard look at herself in the mirror. She looked tired, and she was. By the tone of her voice one would think that she was angry, when actually, she was disappointed and her face showed that, as well. Tyler Martin held such promise. Their first date was almost perfect. The only flaw she remembered was his shirt being wrinkled, but she quickly got over it. Rachel was looking forward to seeing him again. They were actually supposed to go out that night, and that's probably why he sent that picture as a foreshadowing of what was to come. Why did Tyler have to ruin her opinion of him by sending her that stupid picture? It was obvious he didn't respect her. He was looking for a booty call, and she couldn't figure out for the life of her why he would think she was that type of woman. When she met him at the monthly Christian social event she attended and suggested they go out, she thought he would be different from the men she met outside the church. Sadly, he wasn't. *And another one bites the dust,* she thought to herself.

Rachel picked up her phone and looked at the penis picture again. She hadn't seen one of those in a while. What was she doing wrong? She prayed. She read her Bible. She went to church. She volunteered. She kept herself up with exercises and took great care and time with her appearance. She even paid attention to sports and learned how to play poker and shoot pool so she could have more in common with men. Yet she was still single without even a prospect for a boyfriend. Why was it taking Boaz so long to get to her? Did her Boaz get hit by a bus? Maybe he was in some hospital recuperating from his injuries. Maybe he had amnesia and forgot that he was supposed to be on his way to claim his queen. Perhaps his brain injuries were so severe that he now had the intellect of a seven-year-old and was no longer capable of loving her as a man should. She knew she was being silly, but she needed some kind of logical explanation of why she was single.

The last guy Rachel dated said she was moving too fast when she suggested they enter into a relationship after going out for a month, and the one before him said she was too aggressive and clingy. All she wanted was someone to love her and someone to give her love to.

Rachel turned on the faucet. As the cool liquid gushed out, she cupped her hand, closed her eyes, and splashed it on her face. It felt good, but it did nothing to wash away her disappointment. As she reached for a paper towel, she heard the toilet flush. After patting her face dry, she opened her eyes to find the president of the company, Mrs. Finestein, looking directly at her. Rachel was mortified. She had neglected to make sure that no one else was in the restroom before she told Tyler about himself. The old woman had to be deaf not to hear what she said. Rachel hoped she wouldn't mention it.

"That was some conversation you had there, Ms. Hill." Rachel looked down. Hoping had done no good in that instance.

"I'm sorry, Mrs. Finestein. I wasn't aware that anyone was in here. I felt that matter needed to be addressed immediately, and I apologize for taking a personal call on company time. It won't happen again," she said.

Mrs. Finestein was a regal woman of poise and grace. She believed in looking and behaving like a lady. Today, she was wearing a coral-colored suit which she accented with a mother-of-pearl necklace with matching earrings. She could be hard on her employees, but she was usually fair. She made it quite clear in staff meetings that when her employees were at work she expected them to work.

Mrs. Finestein did not acknowledge her apology right away, which caused Rachel to swallow hard. She couldn't afford to lose her job. She had recently purchased a new car, and Felicity needed braces. The older woman proceeded to wash and dry her hands in silence and then she chuckled. "When I was your age, if a man had done something so crass, I would have done more than given him a call. I was a hot-tempered little something in my day. I probably would have went to his home and broken his phone or forwarded the pictures to his mother, asking if that was the sort of thing he was learning at home." She chuckled again. "I actually think you handled it quite well. If you want a man to respect you, you have to demand respect. We are certainly living in a new age. Last week, I confiscated my grandson's phone for bad grades, and I found all kinds of pictures of little girls showing him their breasts and vaginas. Fast-tailed heifers. I was appalled. I had to call my youngest son so he could explain to me about sexting and other nonsense. I wanted to call each of those girls' parents and tell them what they were doing, but on further investigation, I found all kinds of penis pictures from my boy. His grandfather had to have a stern conversation about appropriate and inappropriate behavior, and respecting the opposite sex. The little exhibitionist said it was cool and all his friends did it. I took his phone for a month. We'll see how cool it is now.

"Bless your single heart. If I had to contend with such foolishness, I don't know what I'd do. Men wanting you to send them pictures in your birthday suit. He'd probably show it to all his homies."

Rachel had to smile at her use of the word *homie*. She hadn't heard that since the '90s. Mrs. Finestein continued to empathize with her.

"I could see possibly doing that for your husband. A man you know loves you and will protect your integrity, but someone who you are dating or someone you barely know. That doesn't make sense. You haven't had a chance to determine if he has good character. Heavens, child, I don't envy you single women of today. If my husband asked me for a divorce, I'd probably kill myself. I have no desire to play the dating game at my age."

Mrs. Finestein walked up to Rachel and gave her a hug. "Don't let it get you down. You did the right thing," she said.

Rachel hugged her back. After they released each other, she said, "I'm just so tired of being alone. It seems like because I'm a Christian woman I'm always being overlooked. Men don't want a righteous woman. They want a freak who is acquainted with the church and able to quote scripture."

"It's easy to say you are a Christian. It's harder to behave like it. That's why so many don't. You are saved and set apart. A man whose intentions aren't honorable doesn't deserve to take a seat in your section. Tonight I want you to read your Bible but I also want you to ask yourself this question, 'Should you be waiting on Boaz or should you be waiting on the Lord?' He hears your cries and He hasn't forgotten you. Now fix that face, delete his number and that picture, and get back to work. Those reports aren't going to write themselves."

Rachel smiled at her boss. "Yes, ma'am, and thank you."

"Thank you, darling, for being a rose among thorns. It's going to be okay, I promise you."

Rachel did as she was told. She washed her face, fixed her makeup, and returned to her desk.

That night, Rachel put on her nicest pair of silk pajamas and crawled in between her satin sheets. She liked the way both types of materials felt against her skin. She looked over at the right side of the bed and thought about how nice it would be to have a man over there to hold her. Then she picked up her Bible and turned to chapter 2 in the book of Ruth. Perhaps Ruth and Naomi could give her some encouragement.

[14] At mealtime, Boaz said to her, "Come over here. Have some bread and dip it in the wine vinegar."

When she sat down with the harvesters, he offered her some roasted grain. She ate all she wanted and had some left over. [15] As she got up to glean, Boaz gave orders to his men, "Let her gather among the sheaves and don't reprimand her. [16] Even pull out some stalks for her from the bundles and leave them for her to pick up, and don't rebuke her."

[17] So Ruth gleaned in the field until evening. Then she threshed the barley she had gathered, and it amounted to about an ephah. [18] She carried it back to town, and her mother-in-law saw how much she had gathered. Ruth also brought out and gave her what she had left over after she had eaten enough.

[19] Her mother-in-law asked her, "Where did you glean today? Where did you work? Blessed be the man who took notice of you!"

Then Ruth told her mother-in-law about the one at whose place she had been working. "The name of the man I worked with today is Boaz," she said.

[20] "The Lord bless him!" Naomi said to her daughter-in-law. "He has not stopped showing his kindness to the living and the dead." She added, "That man is our close relative; he is one of our guardian-redeemers."

[21] Then Ruth the Moabite said, "He even said to me, 'Stay with my workers until they finish harvesting all my grain.'"

[22] Naomi said to Ruth her daughter-in-law, "It will be good for you, my daughter, to go with the women who work for him, because in someone else's field you might be harmed."

[2] So Ruth stayed close to the women of Boaz to glean until the barley and wheat harvests were finished. And she lived with her mother-in-law.

3 One day Ruth's mother-in-law Naomi said to her, "My daughter, I must find a home for you, where you will be well provided for. ²Now Boaz, with whose women you have worked, is a relative of ours. Tonight he will be winnowing barley on the threshing floor. ³Wash, put on perfume, and get dressed in your best clothes. Then go down to the threshing floor, but don't let him know you are there until he has finished eating and drinking. ⁴When he lies down, note the place where he is lying. Then go and uncover his feet and lie down. He will tell you what to do."

⁵"I will do whatever you say," Ruth answered. ⁶So she went down to the threshing floor and did everything her mother-in-law told her to do.

⁷When Boaz had finished eating and drinking and was in good spirits, he went over to lie down at the far end of the grain pile. Ruth approached quietly, uncovered his feet and lay down. ⁸In the middle of the night something startled the man; he turned—and there was a woman lying at his feet!

⁹"Who are you?" he asked.

"I am your servant Ruth," she said. "Spread the corner of your garment over me, since you are a guardian-redeemer of our family."

¹⁰"The Lord bless you, my daughter," he replied. "This kindness is greater than that which you showed earlier: You have not run after the younger men, whether rich or poor. ¹¹And now, my daughter, don't be afraid. I will do for you all you ask. All the people of my town know that you are a woman of noble character. ¹²Although it is true that I am a guardian-redeemer of our family, there is another who is more closely related than I. ¹³Stay here for the night, and in the morning if he wants to do his duty as your guardian-redeemer, good; let him redeem you. But if he is not willing, as surely as the Lord lives I will do it. Lie here until morning."

¹⁴So she lay at his feet until morning, but got up before anyone could be recognized; and he said, "No one must know that a woman came to the threshing floor."

¹⁵He also said, "Bring me the shawl you are wearing and hold it out." When she did so, he poured into it six measures of barley and placed the bundle on her. Then he went back to town.

¹⁶When Ruth came to her mother-in-law, Naomi asked, "How did it go, my daughter?"

Then she told her everything Boaz had done for her ¹⁷and added, "He gave me these six measures of barley, saying, 'Don't go back to your mother-in-law empty-handed.'"

¹⁸Then Naomi said, "Wait, my daughter, until you find out what happens. For the man will not rest until the matter is settled today."

Tears began to stream down Rachel's cheeks. She wanted a man like that. A man who was worthy of her and wouldn't rest until he had made her, his. She was tired of being alone, tired of meeting men with dishonorable intentions, and tired of having to call her female or plutonic male friends when she wanted to take a trip, enjoy a concert, and things like that. Those were special outings she wished she could share with someone special. She prayed every night for a husband. She wanted someone with Boaz-like integrity, a good heart, and a desire to provide for her and to keep her safe. She wanted someone to call her own.

As far as Rachel could tell, she was doing the same thing Ruth had done. She was working to take care of herself and her family. She was allowing herself to be visible and approachable. She was living according to the will of God and preparing herself for the time when God would reveal to her the man He had for her. Just like Ruth, Rachel wouldn't be afraid to go to him and offer herself to him as his wife. She was going to wait on God to send her, her Boaz. She really didn't have much choice. Nothing she was doing was working. As Rachel shut her Bible and closed her eyes, there was one question that stayed on her mind. *Does Boaz still exist?*

Heavenly Minded, No Earthly Good

In this meaningless life of mine I have seen both of these: the righteous perishing in their righteousness and the wicked living long in their wickedness. Do not be overrighteous, neither be overwise — why destroy yourself? — Ecclesiastes 7:15 -16

Mary could hear her younger cousins talking about her in the kitchen, but she didn't care. She was a Christian, a woman of God. She was named after the mother of Jesus, for goodness' sake. People talked about Jesus when He was alive, so it only made sense that they would talk about her. Someone had to be concerned about the condition of their souls. It was obvious that they weren't, since they planned this sinful bachelorette party and invited this woman who claimed to be an expert in sexual techniques to talk about all her gadgets, games, and potions designed to heighten the experience in the bedroom—with or without a man. Most of the women there were unmarried, and the only man they needed to be intimate with was Jesus. Those were her thoughts, but Mary didn't say a word. Instead, she stood behind Vivacious Valda as she did her presentation, and gave them all a disapproving glare. The women in the room found it very hard to relax and enjoy themselves. Some of them were interested in Valda's products, but they were too intimidated by Mary to show it. Valda tried to pass around a couple of vibrators and not one of the women present would touch them. Valda grew frustrated. She wondered why they would invite her if they didn't want anything she had to offer.

Mary thought Valda looked like a streetwalker. In her opinion, she wore too much makeup. The glitter above her eyes looked like it belonged on a teenager. Her blouse was cut too low. Her skirt was too short and too tight. A woman with as much behind as she had should wear something loose to hide all that extra seating—not wear something tight to draw attention to it. When Valda pulled out a special spray designed to numb the throat to prevent gagging while performing oral sex, Mary knew it was time for her to speak up.

"I've heard just about enough from you, harlot," she said.

"Excuse, me?" said Valda.

"You call this a Fun Party? There is nothing fun about what you're doing. You are going to send these young women straight to hell with all this talk of orgasms and sexual pleasures. I haven't heard you say one thing about the glorification of our Lord and Savior Jesus Christ. How is any of this going to help these young women get to heaven? I think it's time for you to go." Mary pointed toward the door.

Valda laughed. "Well, I don't know about getting to heaven, but what I have will have them screaming 'Oh God' all night long," she said while moving a huge dildo back and forth in an enclosed hand simulating sex. "Right, ladies?"

The 10 young women in the hotel suite they rented worked hard to stifle their giggles so as not to upset Mary, but none of them said a word.

"Well, I never! You blasphemous—" Mary screamed.

Valda put her hands on her wide hips and smacked her plum-colored lips before cutting her off. "Well, maybe you *should*. That's probably your problem. You need to get laid, lady. Your cooch probably has cobwebs on it. Do you even *have* a man?"

"I'll have you know I've been dating Deacon Theodore Griffin for a little over three months, and we are very happy in Jesus. Our relationship is pure. We abstain from sexual immorality, and we have been blessed for it. Now, I asked you to leave. Your services are no longer needed." Mary picked up a napkin and began placing Valda's items back in her bag, as if touching them was going to give her some type of infection.

A small voice rang out from the couch. "No, Cousin Mary, *you* leave. You are ruining my party. I love you, but you are out of line. My friends and family wanted to do something nice for me before I say I do, and you have made it a disaster. My sisters told me not to invite you, but I didn't want to hurt your feelings. Now, I see that they were right. I am getting married. What's wrong with me learning a few tricks to make sure that I can please my husband in the bedroom? Great sex is one of the perks of marriage. That is one bed that is undefiled. You know that."

Mary stopped placing items in the bag and addressed her little cousin Trinity. She was shocked. Trinity had never spoken to her in such a manner before. "There is nothing wrong with you doing it, but most of your friends are still single. You should have arranged for a private showing. Why would you want to carry on like this in front of others, touching fake penises and such? I thought you knew better."

"News flash, Cousin Mary! Out of all my friends, I am the only one who is still a virgin. They've done a whole lot more than touch a penis," said Trinity.

"Uh-huh, shole have," chimed in Trinity's best friend Kim while giving another young lady a high five. "The D been good to me!"

Mary looked at Kim with a raised eyebrow and said, "Watch your mouth, young lady. I am *still* your elder." She then turned her attention back to Trinity. "You should be proud of your virginity. It's a badge of honor in this sinful, evil world."

Trinity nodded her head. "I am proud, but why do you have to be such a Debbie Downer? You suck the life right out of everything. You make somebody not even want to live saved. God didn't intend for being a Christian to be boring or for Christians to walk around judging everyone else and talk to them in such a condescending tone."

Mary placed her hand on her chest. "I came to look out for you. Are *you* saying I'm boring, young lady?"

"I love you, Cousin Mary, but yes, you *are* boring. With a capital B. All you do is work, pray, go to church, and then repeat . . . work, pray, go to church. There is more to life than those three things. Oh yeah, you also visit the sick. Why don't you go visit some now? Please leave so my friends and I can have some fun. You know what people do at bachelorette parties. If you knew you were going to have a problem with it, then you shouldn't have come. I'm 25 now and fully capable of looking after myself."

Trinity's sisters, Isis and Cleopatra, who were standing behind them in the kitchenette, came out and started clapping. "It's about time you stood up to her. She thinks she can intimidate people with her high and mighty ways and her money. Yeah, it's time for you to step, Cousin. Me and Isis didn't plan this shindig just so you could kill the vibe," said Cleopatra.

"You heard my sister—leave so we can enjoy ourselves!" said Isis.

Mary's feelings were hurt. Trinity was like a daughter to her. She did everything for that girl. She helped pay her tuition when she went off to college at Spelman, and *this* is the thanks she got. She was even paying for some of the expenses associated with her wedding.

Mary went to the chair where she set her purse and jacket and quietly began gathering her things.

"Hey, Sex Lady, pass me that thing you were just holding. I've never seen one that big. I wonder where's that stripper we hired," said Cleopatra.

Mary turned around with her chest puffed out and a huge grin. "Oh, there shall not be any sexually provocative gyrating in here tonight. I sent that enticing serpent home. Luckily, I was in the lobby of the hotel when he arrived. I gave him $50 and sent him on his way, but not before I prayed for him. I think I may have claimed another soul for the kingdom."

"You did what?!" screamed Isis. "I gave that man a $150 deposit! Oh, you better leave and leave now, and you better hope I can get him to come back." Isis then picked up a gigantic vibrator and hurled it at Mary. It hit her smack in the face. Luckily, it had a soft exterior that was designed to feel like skin, so it didn't injure her. Although, the way she reacted one would have thought Isis threw a snake on her.

Mary dropped her things and fell to the floor screaming, "Oh, save me, Jesus! Get it off me! Get it off me! You are going to hell, Isis!"

All the women roared with laughter. Two of them were kind enough to help Mary up, but they were laughing while they did it. Once Mary felt steady on her feet, she stomped on the dildo several times like it was a filthy roach. Because of its circular shape, it moved while she was stepping on it, causing Mary to lose her footing and almost fall again. The women continued to roar with laughter.

"If that's going to send me to hell, then I'll go with a smile on my face. You deserve a lot more than that. You're so heavenly minded, you're no earthy good. No one wants to hear the word from a condescending Bible-thumper like you. Even Jesus had compassion for the unsaved. All you have is disdain. And here's another thing for you . . . Your precious deacon has been screwing Sister Delilah Stewart since before you two started dating. That's why he doesn't care if he gets any from you; he's getting it somewhere else!" screamed Isis.

Mary looked at her with both eyebrows raised and a pointed finger. "Now, *that's* a lie. My Teddy wouldn't be caught dead with that Jezebel. She is a nasty, despicable tramp. She's been with almost every man in the church."

"Bingo!" said Isis and snapped her fingers. "You think she skipped over your precious Teddy? He even came back for seconds, thirds, sixths, fifteenths, and twenty-seconds. Only the good Lord knows how many times he's hit that. He's been making it jiggle, smacking it, flipping it, and rubbing it down, Oh yes! She's sho'nuff giving him something he can feel. Girl, you better put down that holy oil and grab some of this massage oil over here before you lose your man to Jezebel. Ask her what they do late at night while you're in your room alone praying—better yet, ask *him*. I bet he's laying hands all over her."

The room went silent. All the women looked at one another wide-eyed with their lips locked tight. Mary reared back her hand as if she was about to hit Isis but froze with it above her head. Trinity stood up, "Isis, stop it. You've gone too far. Cousin Mary, don't listen to her. She's just mad because you have a good man, and she keeps picking up flea-infested dogs. Let me help you get your things and walk you to your car."

"I almost let the devil cause me to become violent. I'm glad Jesus lives in me. I don't need your help." Mary straightened up her glasses and smoothed out her ankle-length plaid skirt. "I saw myself in here, and I can see myself out." She also ran a hand over her head to make sure that no hairs had escaped the tight bun she wore each day before picking up her items off the floor. "Excuse me for trying to make sure you all get to heaven. I'll say an extra prayer for each of you tonight." She tuned toward Isis. "And you, don't you worry about my relationship. Instead of quoting that sinful R&B, you need to be singing a hymn and praying for salvation, because it is obvious that you are one of the lost." She turned her attention back toward Trinity. "Am I still invited to the wedding?"

"Of course, you are. It wouldn't be the same without you. I love you, and I appreciate everything you have done for me. I'm sorry tonight happened this way. I never meant to hurt your feelings. You go on home. Better yet, call Deacon and see what he's doing. The night is still young; maybe the two of you can go out."

"He's probably doing Sister Stewart," said Cleopatra.

"I said shut up!" barked Trinity.

"It's true, isn't it?" sniffled Mary.

Trinity looked at Mary as her eyes began to turn red and tears threatened to escape. "I've heard rumors, but nobody knows for sure. What I do know is Deacon is a good man, and it is obvious that he is very fond of you." Trinity walked over to her cousin and gave her a warm hug.

"Thank you, Trinity. You always were a sweet girl. You have a good heart. Unlike those hideous sisters of yours. That is why I always gave my money and attention to you. I could tell that you were going to be something. I'm really happy you found a good man."

"Little sister, you better push Mary out of this room before I kick her out—literally," said Isis. "Ain't nothing wrong with the way we turned out. So what if we got kids and live at home with Momma and Daddy? They like being close to their grandkids. We're family, and family takes care of each other," said Isis.

"Yeah," said Cleopatra, nodding her head up and down vigorously.

Trinity looked at her sisters and shook her head from side to side. She loved them dearly, but sometimes they could be so ignorant. It amazed her that the three of them shared the same parents.

"I know, and I love you for it. I needed some better examples. C'mon. Let's go," said Trinity and walked Mary to the door.

On the way home, Mary decided to take a little detour right past Delilah Stewart's house. She knew exactly where she lived. They rotated residences monthly for the women's fellowship meeting, and it had been hosted by Delilah at least twice. She wasn't surprised at all when while looking for the bathroom, she accidently opened her bedroom door and saw a stripper pole over in the corner. Mary never went back to Delilah's home after that. She had no desire to congregate in her den of iniquity.

Mary turned onto Delilah's street and almost rear-ended the car in front of her when she noticed Teddy's car parked out front. She so wanted to believe that he was in there praying for her like he did so many times at church for the other poor lost sinners. She had no intention of merely driving by. She was going to investigate for herself. She wouldn't believe Teddy was cheating on her unless she saw for herself. She parked her car one block over and got out. Mary was glad she wore her flats because she would have had problems running in her usual two-inch heels. She trotted quickly to Delilah's house and crept around to the back. It had rained earlier that day and the ground was soft, so she treaded lightly, trying not to sink into the muddy areas and mess up her shoes. It was around eight o'clock, and the sun had already set. Mary hoped the dark would prevent others from seeing her snooping around Delilah's window.

Mary stood on her tiptoes and looked through the bedroom window. The room was brightly lit. There was slow music playing in the background, but what she saw made her wish she hadn't left her car. Delilah was on her knees in a sheer nightgown, and she definitely wasn't praying, but the man she was pleasuring wasn't Teddy. It was his father, Theodore Griffin, Sr. Mr. Griffin had his head reared back, his eyes closed, and his mouth wide open. She couldn't hear him over the music, but Mary was sure he was moaning and groaning. He looked like he was in paradise. He had one hand behind Delilah's head cradling it, and the other he was using to stroke his right nipple. His breasts were so big he looked as if he needed a bra. His stomach was so huge he looked pregnant. The bottom of it was resting on top of Delilah's head. It was a wonder she could breathe down there. Mary began to feel nauseous. Bile rose up into her mouth. The taste was almost as disgusting as the sight before her. She turned her head and spit it out on the ground beside her. Mr. Griffin was a widower, so he wasn't cheating on Teddy's mother, but Delilah was young enough to be his daughter. Gross! Evidently, he was driving his son's car. Mary was relieved that her man wasn't there, but she didn't know how she was going to purge that sight from her memory. She also didn't know how Teddy would take this news. She *had* to tell him. Mary ran back to her car and drove off. When she was a couple of blocks away, she called her Teddy. He picked up on the first ring.

"Baby, where are you?" she panted.

"I'm at home. My dad's car is in the shop, and I let him borrow mine so I'm kind of stranded. How's the bachelorette party? I miss you." His voice sounded like music to her ears.

"I left. It just wasn't for me. I miss you too. May I come over? Perhaps we can watch a movie. Better yet, let's go out. Why don't we go to that new place you suggested last week where you paint and drink? I think it's called Canvas and Champagne."

Teddy's voice went up two octaves. "Mary? Champagne? But you told me that was Satan's elixir and you wanted no part of it. Are you feeling okay?"

"I could be better. I know what I said, but I've had a change of heart. Baby, drinking alcohol isn't a sin, getting drunk is. You know that. You read the Word just like I do. You think I don't know about those beers you keep in the refrigerator in the garage?"

Deacon chuckled. "Oh, you saw those. I can explain."

"You don't have to. I don't care if you have a beer every now and then, and I don't think God does either. You are a grown man, and I love you."

Teddy paused and smiled. Mary had said the words he had been holding inside. He didn't say them because he was afraid she didn't feel the same. "I love you too. Hurry up and get over here. I don't care what we do as long as I'm with you."

"I feel the same way," said Mary. I'll be there soon. I know I've been a bit stuffy, but I promise to do better."

"Where did that come from? Now, I *know* you have a fever. Yeah, you can be a bit of a Holy Roller at times, but it's your love for Christ that attracted me to you. I've never met a more righteous woman in my life, and that's what I've been praying for. But if you don't mind, can we talk about something other than Jesus and the church sometimes? I love the Lord too, but there are other things in life. That's all we seem to discuss. I actually thought about ending things with you at one point, but the Lord told me that you were the one for me. Instead, I've been praying that you realize that you can loosen up and still be a good Christian woman. It seems like He has answered my prayer. And while you're being less stuffy, can you get your hair done and stop wearing that bun so much? Baby, you have gorgeous hair. Wear it down sometimes. Let me run my fingers through it."

Mary laughed. "You have a lot of requests. I'll see what I can do. You are an answer to my prayers too. Teddy, I prayed for a good man who could appreciate my love for the Lord and wouldn't pressure me for sex. I thought one would never come, and now that you're here, I couldn't imagine life without you. Thank you for not giving up on me. I think those are reasonable requests. Tonight, we will not talk about church, and next week, I'll go to the salon and get a new hairstyle. Now, may I ask you a question without you getting offended?"

"Ask me anything, love," said Teddy.

"Have you ever dated Delilah Stewart?"

"What? No. She started those rumors years ago when I turned down her advances. That woman was after me bad. Once she even showed up to my house when I was sick with some chicken noodle soup. I let her in and took the soup to the kitchen. Next thing I knew, she was standing in my living room in some lingerie."

"No, she wasn't! The *nerve* of that woman. What did you do?" That revelation made Mary want to return to Delilah's house and slash the tires on her car.

"I got her good, baby. I broke out my Bible and started reading it like she wasn't even there. Then she started twerking. I wasn't turned on at all. She's only in her 30s, but that body looks like it's been ran through, over, and under. She had so many stretch marks on her booty and breasts that she reminded me of a zebra. She smacked the Bible out my hand and tried to straddle me. There was no way she was putting that nasty body on me. I jumped up and started shouting, 'Satan, I rebuke you in the name of Jesus!' Then, I grabbed my mother's tambourine and started singing 'Stomp out de Devil' like she wasn't there. Delilah got mad. I mean *real* mad. She cussed me out, accused me of liking men, and left. She even took her chicken soup with her. It didn't matter.

That woman is nasty, I wasn't going to eat anything she cooked. The next thing I knew, she had spread rumors all 'round the church that we were intimate on a regular basis. A woman like that could never entice me. I like my woman chaste and ladylike with smooth caramel skin like my Berry Mary. Are you on your way, yet?" he cooed.

"Yes, baby. I'm about 10 minutes away," said Mary. "That is hilarious. I can't believe Delilah was brazen enough to do that." She was still contemplating whether she should tell Teddy about his father and Delilah. "Did your father tell you where he was going?"

"Naw. He just said he had something to do. No telling knowing him. Since Mother died, I just let him do his thang."

"I see."

"Why do you ask?"

"Oh, no reason."

Mary decided that it wasn't her place to tell Teddy that his father was sleeping with Delilah. She knew he held his father in high regard. She would pray for Mr. Griffin and asked the Lord to deliver him from the snares of a temptress and protect him from sexually transmitted diseases. She shuddered as the sight of him naked crept back into her thoughts. She would even pray for Delilah and her deliverance from sexually immorality but she better stay away from her Teddy! Mary was glad they were going to Canvas and Champagne because after a night like tonight, she *needed* a drink.

Live A Little

May he give you the desires of your heart and make all your plans succeed. – Psalms 20:4

"I don't understand why I'm single," said Monica. "I'm attractive. I'm financially stable, so I don't need a man to come save me or pay my bills. I'm intelligent. I think I'm a great catch. Why do I see all these needy, unattractive chicks with a man, but I can't seem to buy a date."

"That is not true. Men ask you out all the time. You always turn them down," said her younger sister Sasha. "Turn the air on; it's hot in here."

Monica reached in front of her and turned on the air-conditioning in her car. It was going to take a few minutes to get really cold so her sister would have to suffer a little longer. "I do not count the boy at the drive-through window, nor my mechanic or the guy who cleans my building as viable options. Is it too much to want someone who isn't still battling pimples or on my payroll?"

"See, that's your problem right there. You are too doggone picky. You are 40 years old, which means your options aren't as great as they used to be. You forget that you are competing with 20- and 30-year-olds who want the same thing you do—a good man. Add that to the fact that there aren't that many around because most of them are already married, gay, or in jail, and you are at even more of a disadvantage. It's like those TVs they sell on Black Friday. There's a line around the building, but

they only have 15 TVs. You need to lower your standards, big sis. If he's gainfully employed, isn't a pathologi-
cal liar, and looks reasonably attractive, snatch him up.
Besides, you're *always* working. When do you have time
for a man anyway? You only have yourself to blame. You
are the one who put your love life on hold because you
wanted to get an education and build an empire. I am
quite proud of your career accomplishments, but now
you are suffering the consequences of that decision."

Monica looked at her sister. She was using both
hands to fan herself. Sasha was five months pregnant
and absolutely glowing. She had been with her husband
Samuel since they were in the eighth grade. If only she
had been as lucky to find her forever love when her
biggest dilemmas were what to wear to class and an
upcoming test.

"I will not settle for less than what I deserve just so I
can say I have a man. I'd make time if I had a beau, but I
don't have anyone, so I work to fill the time. Please don't
blame my ambition on my lack of eligible bachelors.
SheFyre is one of the fastest-growing online magazines in
the country. Do you know how much I make on ads
alone? I've got 500,000 readers worldwide and to create
content that keeps them engaged takes time, hard work,
and dedication."

Sasha looked at her sister. She just didn't get it.
"True but at what cost. You have your dream house,
dream car, and dream career—and no one to share it
with, not even a dog. Newsflash, honey, you have to
mingle if you want to stop being single. That means
going somewhere other than the grocery store. Broaden
your horizons."

"I don't like dogs, and I don't like going to the grocery store. I have a personal shopper who does that for me," said Monica.

"See what I mean? Stop being so bourgeois. The only men you see are the preacher and the mailman. Pastor Gibson is already happily married, and I've seen your mailman. He's probably got grandchildren older than you."

Monica had to laugh at the thought of getting with Mr. Baker. He should have retired years ago. He said the exercise was good for him, and he had no desire to sit around the house looking at Mrs. Baker all day. "You're right. Maybe I should complain to the post office that I need a younger postal carrier in my neighborhood," she joked.

"That is not my point, and you know it! You need to get out and do things so you can meet someone. You already said yourself that you're a great catch, but no one would know it because no one sees you. If I weren't your hairstylist, I'd probably never see you," said Sasha. "You could try online dating. Goodness, it's hot! Help me take off this jacket." Sasha held out her arm, and Monica grabbed the cuff of the black cotton blazer she was wearing and pulled.

"No way! There are too many crazies on the 'net. They get you out of your comfort zone and then rape or kill you. I want my first meeting with my potential husband to be face-to-face. I'm not really that picky. I've had the same list of requirements since college. He has to be my height or taller with a nice smile. He has to be gainfully employed with a job that pays at least $75,000 a year. He has to be smart and funny with a great sense of style. He also has to treat his mother well, because if a man will mistreat his mom, he won't think twice about mistreating his woman."

Sasha shook her head while she shimmied her arm out of one sleeve and then relieved her heated body of the other. "Thanks, Big Sis. See, there you go again being all picky. What have all these rules and that list gotten you? NOTHING! You've got to show your face for someone to see it. I have an idea! There's this great new lounge that just opened called Luxury. We should go. There are bound to be some eligible bachelors there."

"I don't know . . ." said Monica.

Her sister put up her finger and rolled her neck like they used to do as teenagers. "Look, Missy, do you want my help or not? Keep doing what you're doing and before long your breasts will sag to your knees, you'll be missing some of your teeth, and the only men you'll be able to attract are the ones in the nursing home with you. Can you say erectile dysfunction and hanging balls? My friends told me about Luxury last week. You'll love it. They have live music. I hear the band is great and the lead singer is hot."

Sasha knew how much Monica loved live music so that definitely piqued her interest. But as far as she was concerned, lounge was just the mature and sexy way to say nightclub, and she outgrew those in college. However, if there was a band there, she could focus on them instead of any men who walked up to her with lame pickup lines. She also had to admit that her little sister was right. She needed to get out of the house. Her last three weekends had been spent home on the couch watching movies. The air was blowing cooler now, and Sasha looked a little more comfortable.

"Okay, I'll go," she said.

"Fantastic. I'll get the details together and shoot them to you. I'm also going to come over and help you pick out your wardrobe."

"What? No. I don't need—"

"Girl, please. You've been off the scene so long, your trendy clothes expired years ago. I'm going to come over to make sure your ensemble is something from this decade."

Monica looked down at her clothing. The jeans she was wearing did come from the thrift store she found while vacationing in Chicago a few years ago. Her shirt was a plain black turtleneck. She could have passed for the black female Steve Jobs. Rest his soul. She wished she had his money, though. Running Apple was quite a lucrative business.

"Okay, but you will not make me look like one of those cougars with all their cleavage out trying to pick up 20-year-old college students hoping to get their tuition paid."

Sasha held up three fingers and said, "Scouts honor. I couldn't do that anyway, 'cuz you don't have cleavage." She grabbed her enlarged breasts with both hands and lifted them up. "*These* are breasts. *You* have knots."

Monica balled up her napkin and threw it at Sasha. "I see you're feeling yourself since those milk jugs are finally helping to give you a shape. But your backside could still be used for a tabletop if you bent over. Besides, I'm proud of my girls. A size 36B is average. Not too big and definitely not too small. They're not bothering you, so why are you bothering them? No man I've dated has ever complained."

"That's because they haven't been introduced to the land of plenty," Sasha said waving her hands around her chest. "But I'm sure there will be a man there who doesn't know any better."

They laughed. Both sisters enjoyed their friendly competitive banter. They had a wonderful relationship and treasured it greatly. That day they decided to meet for a quick bite and then went over to check out a new store in one of the shopping centers near the restaurant. They were now sitting in Monica's car and chatting for a bit before they had to part ways.

"I've got to get back to the shop. Old Lady Shea is my next client. She's a mean old coot, but she's a great tipper," said Sasha.

Sasha was a hairstylist at Indulge Salon and Spa, and a pretty good one at that. She was usually booked weeks in advance.

"I'll see you in an hour, girl," said Monica.

"Oh, I forgot that you're coming to see me today. Fantastic! I can whip that mane into shape before we go find you a man."

Monica threw another napkin at her sister before Sasha exited her car and walked to her own.

An hour later, Monica walked into the salon as promised. Sasha was putting Mrs. Laura O'Shea of the prestigious O'Shea family under the dryer. The O'Sheas owned a successful commercial property company and several other businesses in the city. They, along with their millions, were well-known.

"I am not pleased, young lady. I was here on time, and I expect you to be as well," the elderly lady scolded Sasha.

"I apologize, AGAIN, Mrs. O'Shea, but I got a flat tire on my way back to the salon. Thankfully, a nice man stopped and changed my tire or I would have been even later. Roadside assistance said it would be an hour before they could get to me. He even let me sit in his brand new Mercedes with ice-cold air-conditioning while he changed it."

"It's M*iss*, Sasha. I am not married, nor do I want to be. Single, no kids, and happy about it." The tone she used to correct Sasha was quite nasty. Monica wondered what in the world could be so wrong with being married with children.

"That's because no man could put up with you," she muttered.

"What was that, dear?" the old lady shouted from under the dryer.

"I was just singing to myself." She looked in Monica's direction and motioned for her to come closer with her head. "Looks like you need a retouch. How do you feel about adding a few highlights to brighten you up a little bit?"

Monica looked at Sasha like she had lost her mind and put her face as close to hers as she could without kissing her. "You better not. I'll move every piece of furniture in the place while I whip you and that baby's behind," she whispered.

Sasha loved to joke with Monica about her natural hair. Monica was fiercely loyal to her kinky, coily hair. She considered it an extension of her personality—full of beauty and hard to tame.

Sasha giggled. "How about we do something different and flat iron your hair?"

"No way!" Monica sat down in the chair, looked in the mirror, and patted her afro.

Sasha draped a plastic cape around her. "It's not like it's going to stay that way. Live a little. You said you wanted something different, so try something different. I'm tired of seeing this afro all the time. What about the color I mentioned?"

Monica bit her bottom lip. "No, but I will let you do some type of roller set. I normally only let you twist or braid it."

Sasha behaved like she had won the lottery. "Deal! This is exciting. I'm going to make you gorgeous, girl."

She sent Monica to the shampoo tech in the washing area near the back of the salon. There were already several women seated at the shampoo bowls patiently waiting. Monica hated when Sasha sent her to the shampoo tech because there was only one, and she took forever. Sasha must have somehow felt her unhappy vibes because a few minutes later she came in the room and washed Monica's hair herself. She then applied some conditioner, put on a plastic cap, and set her under the dryer next to Old Lady Shea. She was no longer under the dryer hood, but was sitting on the edge of the seat, fanning herself profusely. Her face was flushed and sweat was forming at her temples.

"Are you okay?"

"I'll be okay. It's just these darn hot flashes. You'd think at 75 years old I'd be rid of them, but I still get them every now and then. I don't know why they decided to attack me while I was under the dryer."

Monica stood up and said, "My sister has been hot a lot lately too, but her internal heat is due to pregnancy. Let me get you some water."

"Thank you, dearie."

Monica walked over to a nearby water cooler and filled two small cone cups. She returned to Old Lady Shea and barely reached her hand toward her when the woman snatched the first cone out of her hand and downed it quickly. The second one was for herself, but after witnessing her thirst, Monica offered that one as well. Old Lady Shea reached more kindly for it and drank it a little more slowly.

"Thank you, that is so much better."

While she was drinking, the nail technician, Shakina, came over and had a seat with them. She and Monica had known each other for years, and whenever she was in the salon, Shakina would try to find a moment to come chat with her. They acknowledged each other with a smile and a head nod.

"*Miss* O'Shea," said Monica, emphasizing the "Miss," "when I came in, I heard you talking about the fact that you are unmarried with no kids and you are proud of it. Please excuse me for eavesdropping, but may I ask why you never got married?"

Old Lady Shea seemed to sit up a little straighter at the question and proudly answered, "I couldn't find anyone worthy of me. My father treated me like a princess, and I needed a man who was capable of doing the same. Look at me. You can't look like this on a bus driver's salary. I wanted, as you kids say, 'a baller.' My father was the epitome of a well-to-do, refined gentleman. I couldn't seem to find a man who was charming, handsome, *and* rich, and I refused to settle. Oh, I had plenty of suitors. One was that bus driver I mentioned. Another was an investment banker. He had plenty of money, but he was fat and his breath smelled like the dickens. He was nice enough, I suppose, but who wants some bear sweating all over them in the bedroom. I was quite a beauty in my day, and I needed a man to complement that."

"Couldn't you have encouraged him to lose weight and gotten him some mouthwash?" Monica asked.

Old Lady Shea put a little attitude in her demeanor and a smile on her face. "Honey, I don't do fixer-upper cars, houses, or men. You need to have yourself together to be with me."

"I hear you, Miss Shea. Men today don't know how to treat a lady anyway. All they wanna do is take you out to get in your panties. Like dinner at Olive Garden is supposed to tempt you to give it up. You have no idea how many men with girlfriends and wives try to talk to me on a daily basis. It really is sad. A good man is sho'nuff hard to find. I don't blame you at all for tapping out," said Shakina.

Monica had more questions, but she wasn't sure if she should continue to pry in a stranger's life. However, she needed answers and decided to proceed. "Hmm . . . Don't you want someone? I mean, just for companionship?"

"I have a successful business that provides for all of my needs, no matter how extravagant they may be, Jesus, and my cats. And all nine of them are male and provide excellent company."

Monica could not have hidden the shock on her face if she wanted to. "Nine?"

"Oh yes. Samson, Cyrus, Lionel, Vernon, Ralph, Ronnie, Bobby, Ricky, and Mike. As you can tell, I used to love New Edition back in the day. They were the cutest boys, and they grew up to be handsome young men. My cats are all the men I need. They sleep in my bed and keep me warm at night. They don't talk back, question my authority to make decisions with my money, or tell me what I need to cook for dinner. I encountered all that rubbish when I was dating. I was even engaged once. He was handsome and intelligent but hadn't realized his financial potential yet. I was willing to stand by him and even get my father to invest in his vision. In the meantime, I had every intention of living off my family's money. He wouldn't hear of it. That fool got mad when I took back the cheap ring he bought me and exchanged it for something better. He said I wanted to wear the pants in the relationship and that I emasculated him. I don't see what the problem was. I was the one who had to wear it, and I paid for the upgrade with my money. It didn't cost him a dime."

Shakina laughed. "C'mon, Miss Shea, you've got to have a man somewhere. They are good for something. Taking out the trash, killing large bugs, and fixing on cars. What do you do when you get the urge to scratch that good lovin' itch?"

"My dear, when you're my age, 'scratching itches,' as you say, are no longer a priority, but in my prime, I could always get a lover if I needed one. When you are beautiful with money, you'll never have a problem getting a man. I never had a shortage of dates. I had a shortage of suitable mates." Old Lady Shea laughed. "Some of the biggest playboys in the city were at my beck and call, but they were only good for warming my bed. I knew that if I ever married one of them, they would run through my money and leave me penniless. My father wouldn't have had that anyway. Daddy always did look out for me. A well-to-do woman has to be careful."

Monica took a good look at Old Lady Shea while she talked. Her makeup was flawless, and it was obvious that her clothing was designer, but she was covered in cat hair. The fine hairs showed up clearly on the black slacks she was wearing, and they were multiple colors and different lengths. No wonder she was alone. No man was going to deal with that. Looking at it made Monica want to sneeze and find a lint brush, and she didn't have allergies. She wondered if Miss Shea was really happy being by herself or was that something she convinced herself to believe in order to feel better. She didn't know and wouldn't insult the woman by asking, but there was one thing Monica did know. She didn't want to be like her: old, alone, and covered in feline hair sprinkled with dander.

Shakina kept talking. "I feel you. When my ex, Sebastian, found out I made enough to stay off welfare, he thought he was going to stay home and babysit my 60-inch TV. He tried to feed me some lie about he was waiting for his disability to get approved. I put that tail out. Well, my next client is here. It was good talking to you. Monica, when Sasha is done with your hair, come see me so we can do a fill-in and polish change."

As she walked off, Sasha appeared from the shampoo room with another other client and said, "Let me wrap her hair and I'll be right with you, girl."

"No rush," said Monica. She was fine sitting there with Miss Shea and her thoughts. Was she really alone because she was too picky and bourgeois like her sister said? She did have standards, but she didn't think she was as bad as Miss Shea. How did any woman expect a man to be okay with taking his ring back? He probably got her what he could afford and was proud of it. Monica didn't want just a lover to warm her bed. She wanted a man who was her husband, best friend, and lover to warm her heart. She suddenly had visions of herself as an elderly woman dining in a restaurant alone with families and couples seated all around her. She looked pathetic and sad.

"Monica! Monica!" She realized that someone was calling her name and looked up to find Sasha standing over her.

"Big Sis, are you going deaf? Didn't you hear me? What in the world are you thinking about?"

Monica looked over at Miss Shea who was now back under the dryer hood and dozing off.

"I don't want to end up old and alone," she said.

"Girl, stop saying that. Don't speak negativity in the atmosphere. You've got a lot of good years left in you, and there is a man out there who wants to share them with you. Now, come let me do that hair so you can turn some heads. *Operation: Snag Monica A Man* is now in full effect."

Sasha grabbed Monica by the hand, danced her over to the shampoo bowl, and washed out the conditioner. Monica then had a seat in her styling chair, where Sasha began applying products before parting and rolling her hair. The bell chimed, indicating that someone was entering the salon. Everyone looked around to see an attractive black man in a business suit striding through the door toward them. Sasha's eyes lit up, and her face upturned into a huge smile.

"Stanley, what are you doing here?"

"Sasha, you left your lipstick in my car," he replied.

"Did I? It must have fallen out of my purse when I was digging in it. Thank you for bringing it. It's my favorite color."

"No problem. I looked at the business card you gave me and realized that I had to come in your neck of the woods for a meeting and decided to drop it off. Who is this vision of loveliness sitting in your chair?" he said while directing his attention toward Monica.

Stanley was staring at her with a nice smile adorned with thick, delicious-looking lips that he casually licked. He had incredibly smooth skin. It reminded Monica of whipped chocolate mousse. Monica became very self-conscious. She was definitely not looking her best. All she was wearing was lip gloss and her hair was all over her head. Several other women in the salon were ogling Stanley and hoping he would look in their direction. However, Monica seemed to have his full attention.

"This is my sister, Monica," said Sasha. "Monica, this is Stanley. The man who helped me change my tire today."

Monica realized that she had no place to run so she decided the best thing to do was flash her winner smile and be polite. She extended her hand and said, "It's a pleasure to meet you. Thank you for taking care of my baby sister. I hate the thought of her being stranded on the side of the road in her condition. You changed her tire in a suit?"

"He sure did," piped in Sasha.

"I'm impressed," said Monica. "Most men would have kept going so they wouldn't have to get dirty."

Stanley was still holding her hand and seemed to be in no hurry to let it go. "I was taught to never leave a woman in distress. I love your hair, by the way. You and your sister are both natural beauties. Pardon my quick departure, but I must get back to work. It was a pleasure meeting you, Monica, and it was nice to see you again, Sasha. Make sure you get a new tire and get off that donut as soon as you can." He released Monica's hand.

"I will," said Sasha. "Thank you, again, and if there is anything I can do for you, please let me know. Be safe out there."

"I most certainly will, madam. You do the same. Keep looking beautiful, Monica."

Monica smiled bashfully and said, "I'll do my best."

Stanley bowed and left.

"Giirl, I think he was feeling you," squeaked Sasha.

Monica tried to act nonchalant about it. "He was just being polite."

Sasha shook her head. "You've been off the dating scene so long you don't even know when a man is interested. So sad. Tsk, tsk, tsk."

"Girl, shut up and whip my hair. I have to catch my-self a husband before my ovaries turn to dust." Sasha laughed and got back to work on her sister's hair.

Two days later, Sasha and Monica met at Luxury for drinks and music. Sasha looked out of place with her protruding baby bump, but she knew if she didn't come, Monica wouldn't either. The lounge was really nice. It had high, vaulted ceilings with hanging fans to keep dancers cool. The décor contained several panels of etched glass. Those who chose to have a seat could do so at one of several mahogany tables surrounded by cush-ioned chairs. The VIP was home to several glass tables and black and red leather couches and chairs.

As Monica passed by one of the wall mirrors, she caught a glimpse of herself. The curls Sasha did for her framed her small face perfectly. She approved of the outfit her sister assembled for her by blending her favorite hot pink top with a flouncy black skirt Sasha could no longer fit. It, along with her black sequined heels, showed off her toned legs. She felt sexy, stylish, and classy. Sasha wore a simple black-and-white, striped, baby-doll dress with silver heels. Monica and Sasha had a seat at one of the mahogany tables. Sasha drank cranberry juice while Monica sipped on a mojito. The two got there early to make sure they were able to get a good seat to hear the band. There weren't a lot of people there when they arrived, but within an hour the place was packed. The band was playing a funky groove everyone seemed to enjoy. Her sister was right. The lead singer was extremely sexy. He was belting out a song by Tyrese that had almost every woman in the place on her feet. Monica was enjoying the band so much she barely noticed when Stanley walked up and stood right in front of her. He was dressed a little more casual than before in khaki pants and a yellow cotton button-down shirt, but he still looked good. It was obvious that he had gotten a fresh cut and shave. Monica definitely liked what she saw.

His delectable lips moved to say, "Do you mind if I join you two ladies?"

"Not at all," cooed Sasha.

Monica gave her sister the evil eye. She had been set up, and she knew it. The two ladies made room for Stanley at their table. He ordered a drink for himself and another one for each of them. They made light conversation between the three of them while listening to the band. After finishing her second drink, Sasha said she had to leave. She gave some lame excuse about the baby leaning on her bladder and she needed to go home so she could pee repeatedly in peace. Monica didn't mind, though. Sasha stayed long enough for her to feel comfortable around Stanley. She actually welcomed a little one-on-one time with him.

The club was now in full swing. The band was playing popular cover songs, and the dance floor was crowded with people trying to shake off the stress of the workday. After Sasha left, Stanley moved his chair closer to Monica so they could hear each other more clearly over the music.

He leaned into her and said, "I didn't think it was possible but you look lovelier tonight than the day I met you." Monica could feel the warm breath escaping from between those luscious lips on her neck. It sent a slight tingle through her body.

She blushed. "Thank you, Stanley. You look pretty nice yourself. I must say, I'm surprised to see you here."

He took his hand and moved a stray hair from her face. His index finger lightly touched her temple and sent more tingles through her. "Can I tell you a secret?" he said.

She turned toward him. He face was dangerously close to hers, "Yes, I'm good at keeping secrets."

"I called your sister and asked about you. When she told me you were single, I asked her if she could arrange another meeting. She told me you two were coming here tonight and suggested I stop by. I'm glad I did."

"Me, too." Sasha could barely believe that this attractive man who rescued a pregnant damsel in distress was interested in her. And to think that her family was trying to convince her to lower her standards. Right now, Stanley seemed to fulfill every requirement on her list, although she had to talk to him a little more to figure out what his spiritual life was like and if he loved his mother.

Monica wanted to say something else, but she wasn't quite sure what. Stanley's attractive frame, intoxicating cologne, and seductive voice had her struggling to find something intelligent talk about. Maybe words weren't needed. They both seemed content staring into each other's eyes for the time being. They were so engrossed in each other that neither of them saw two uniformed police officers approach their table.

The male officer cleared his throat and said, "Excuse me. Are you Stanley Green?"

Stanley broke his gaze from Sasha and smiled nervously. "Why, yes, I am."

"Good. You're under arrest for identity theft." The female officer came behind them and instructed Stanley to stand. He did as he was told, and she placed him in handcuffs. Sasha was stunned.

"Officers, do we have to do this in front of the lady and the other patrons?" Stanley's eyes pleaded with them to allow him some grace.

"Okay, Playboy, we can finish this outside," said the first officer.

"Walk," said the other officer and turned Stanley's body and hers toward the door. She took one step and then stopped to address Monica. "Miss, consider yourself lucky. This man is notorious for wining and dining ladies and then robbing them blind."

Monica looked at Stanley, hoping he would say something to defend himself. This had to be a mistake. He couldn't even look at her in her eyes. He offered no explanation but simply said, "Sorry to ruin our evening, lovely lady." The officer pushed him toward the exit. Monica was once again struggling to find words, but it wasn't in a good way. She couldn't believe what was happening. Several people were staring in her direction, so she decided to abandon her table and head to the bar. She now needed something stronger than a mojito.

"Hello," said the bartender. "What can I get you?"

"A shot of Patrón please," she said, looking around to see if people were still staring at her. Most of them appeared to have returned to listening to the band. They were now performing a fast song by Usher. Monica had never had Patrón, but the last time she went out, several of her friends ordered shots of it, and she figured now was as good a time as ever to try it.

"Really? You don't look like a shot kind of girl," he said.

"Usually, I'm not, but I need something to help me forget that I'm 40 years old, single, and the gentleman I was with tonight just got arrested for identity theft," said Monica.

"Oh yeah. I saw that. That's a horrible way to spend the evening. The first one's on the house. You look like you need it."

"Thanks." The bartender set the shot in front of Monica She picked it up, downed it in one gulp, and slammed the glass down on the counter. It had a strong taste she wasn't accustomed to that left a burning sensation in the back of her throat and chest. She didn't like it but she hoped it would help her forget about her nonexistent love life. She coughed and said, "Hit me again."

The bartender handed her a wedge of lime to chase it with. She sucked on it quickly. "Slow down, pretty lady. I want you to be able to walk out of here." He looked at her with concern, which Monica mistook for pity. She didn't want anyone's pity. What she wanted was another drink.

She removed the lime from her mouth. "Thanks but my father is at home watching the evening news. Hit me again, please."

"As you wish," he said pouring another and setting it in front of her. Monica downed that one as fast as the first and slammed down the glass once again. Then she held out her hand for another lime.

She took a good look at the bartender, who was now looking at her with a smirk on his face. He was a cute, light-skinned guy. The stubble he was allowing to grow on his face made him sexy in a rugged kind of way. He looked to be close to her age. She finished sucking the lime he gave her and said, "Tell me something, Bartender," said Monica.

"The name's Doug," he said. "But ask anything you like."

"Sorry. Well, tell me something, Doug, what makes a man look right past a women who has two degrees, a successful, home-based business, and no kids? I'm perfect wife material."

"I can't speak for all men, but I know for me, it would be that she is too busy spouting off her credentials to know that a man is more interested in whether she can hold a decent conversation, cook, likes sports, and if she'll be a good mother to any future children."

"What? Seriously?" said Monica.

"Yep. A man who is looking for a wife has already put himself in a position to be able to take care of her, so he won't care about her credentials. Don't get me wrong, we want an intelligent woman who makes her own money, but there are lots of millionaires without degrees. I don't have a degree, and I do well. If I saw a woman like you, I would ask her out, but I'd be turned off if we went out, and all she wanted to talk about was her degrees and why she's still single."

Before Monica knew she said it, the words fell out of her mouth. "Great. Then it's a date." She wondered what was in that Patrón. It must alter the drinker's brain cells and make them do something they normally wouldn't do. Monica never asked men out. She believed it was the man's job to pursue the woman. But what would it hurt? There wasn't exactly anyone kicking down her door for a date with her at the moment.

"You mean you want to go out with a bartender with no college degree?" he said.

"Why not? My father didn't have a degree and he took great care of us on his maintenance worker salary. I need a man who knows how to treat a woman and is ready to settle down. Now back to you. You're alive. You're cute. You have a job, and at your age, you probably don't need Viagra yet. Besides, my sister says I should relax and live a little. So what do you say, Doug, the bartender? Would you like to go out with me and live a little?" she said seductively. That Patrón was really causing her to be bold, or so she told herself.

"I'd love to, but I'm not a bartender. Well, not usually. I'm the owner of this beautiful establishment. I'm bartending tonight because I have one out sick. And I lied. I actually have an MBA from Dartmouth. I wanted to see what you would say when I told you I didn't have a degree, and lucky for you, I'm in the market for a great girlfriend who I might be able to one day make my wife."

Monica smiled. "Lucky for you I'm a huge sports fan, I like to cook, can hold a decent conversation, and would make a great mother."

Doug smiled. "I've got tickets to the Chicago Bulls game for Monday night. Would you like to accompany me, Monica?"

"How do you know my name?" She knew she hadn't told him.

"Your sister told me when she was waiting for you to arrive. I was hoping you would come to the bar. I think you are absolutely gorgeous. I wasn't going to say anything when I saw you with that guy, but it appears he is no longer a problem."

Monica laughed. "You're right. I don't do thieves. I'd love to go to the game with you, Doug." Monica sat back on her stool and smiled and tried to play it cool, but inside, she was screaming, YEEEEEES!

******

One year later, Monica and Doug got married. She owed it all to her sister, an identity thief, and a magic elixir she never partook of again after the night they met.

Find the Humor In It

But he's already made it plain how to live, what to do, what God is looking for in men and women. It's quite simple: Do what is fair and just to your neighbor, be compassionate and loyal in your love, and don't take yourself too seriously - take God seriously. — Micah 6:8

Emily sat in the lounge on a bar stool awaiting the arrival of her best friend and her date. Neither one seemed to understand the concept of being on time. Pam was supposed to be her escape plan in case her date, whom she met online, turned out to be far less attractive than the pictures he posted on his profile. The restaurant he suggested was beautiful, so even if he was unattractive, he had good taste. The place possessed the perfect ambiance for a romantic evening, which could also prove to be an annoyance if her date was not her type. The lights were dim. A pianist was playing soft music nearby. Lovers were cuddling on several plush gray sofas, smiling in one another's faces and quietly conversing. A few were even sneaking soft kisses in here and there. *Where is Pam?* thought Emily. She was the only reason Emily signed up for an online dating site, and her friend promised she would be there to bail her out if her first date went to the left. She wiggled on her barstool in an attempt to get comfortable.

"The only thing that girl is going to be on time for is her funeral, and that's because someone else will be escorting her there," Emily muttered under her breath.

Her phone was sitting face-up on the table in front of her. It vibrated, indicating that she had a text message. "That better not be Pam saying she is not going to make it," she said aloud, as if someone were sitting next to her listening.

Emily looked down to find a message from her date, Brody. It read, TURN AROUND.

And turn around she did, and she found herself staring face to chest with a humongous man. He could best be described as the black version of the popular 1980s wrestler André the Giant. Emily felt a wave of panic wash over her. She laughed nervously and then tilted her head upward to see his face. Brody was handsome, but not an exact resemblance of the picture he posted. That man was buff. He looked like a bodybuilder. The only thing this man looked like he lifted was his fork and probably a few cupcakes. Although the face could match the ones in the photos, if you extracted the large jaws that were probably a result of the weight gain. Emily didn't know quite what to say, so she continued to look up in awe.

"You must be Emily," the gargantuan said with a nice, broad smile that revealed a very nice set of white teeth, and nestled in those fat cheeks were two dimples.

Emily didn't say a word, but continued to smile before looking frantically to her left and then her right. She wanted to curse out the manager for allowing such dim lighting. She could barely see clearly farther than five feet. Where in the world was Pam to save her? Emily didn't see her, and she had to think fast. She could lie but that wouldn't work. She told Brody what she was going to be wearing and how she was going to style her hair. Besides, she had looked at her phone and turned around after receiving his text. To lie would just be plain mean, and she truly believed in treating people like she wanted to be treated. Also, if he were the violent type, he could easily smack her into the wall behind the bar and then kick her into oblivion.

"Uuhh . . . yeah. And you must be Brody," said Emily. She wished he would take a step back.

"Yes. It's a pleasure to meet you, and if you don't mind me saying, you are beautiful." Brody gave her a warm, genuine hug as if he were really happy she was there.

Emily suddenly relaxed. There were worst places she could be than in an elegant restaurant with an obese man who thought she was beautiful. Big men weren't her type, but it was only dinner. "You have no idea how long it's been since I've heard that. Thank you," she said.

"You're welcome. I checked with the hostess before I came to find you and our table is ready. I hope you're hungry, because I'm starving." *I bet you are,* thought Emily. She reached into her Tory Burch bag and left money on the table to pay for her Perrier water. Brody extended a rather large arm for her to hold. She hesitated for a minute. The last thing she wanted was for someone to think that they were together, as in an item or couple. Yet, it wasn't like she was with anyone at all. She hadn't had a boyfriend in years and a decent date in months.

After Emily slid off her stool she was able to get a better view of him. Brody was wearing grey slacks and a brown belt. His humongous belly lapped over the belt to the point that it was barely visible from the front. He also wore a white dress shirt with grey stripes. You could see his white T-shirt underneath his unbuttoned collar. Sticking out above the shirt were several curly black hairs. His cuffs were held together by two bejeweled cuff links adorned with the letter B. His brown shoes were leaning on their sides. The task of upholding someone that huge seemed to be a little more than they could handle, and they were buckling under the pressure. Brody was big, but he was confident and his demeanor was kind and welcoming. She would describe his attire as decent. Emily thought for a restaurant of this caliber, it would have been more appropriate had he worn a suit coat.

Brody noticed her apprehension. "Don't worry. I won't bite. Although, you do look good enough to eat," Brody said with a chuckle.

Emily hoped she wouldn't see anyone she knew as she reached out and grabbed his meaty arm. Brody escorted her to the front of the restaurant, and when the hostess saw him, she immediately grabbed two menus from behind her stand and escorted them to their table. Brody pulled out the chair for Emily and waited for her to get comfortably seated before walking to his own chair and seating himself.

"This was a nice selection," said Emily. "I have never been here. I Googled it before I came. It has a nice atmosphere, good menu selection, and reasonable prices." She opened the menu and started eyeing it.

"I love this place. They serve the best steaks," said Brody without looking up from his menu.

"I see they have pasta. I think I'm going to try that," she said.

"Let me suggest their Cajun pasta. The seafood is always fresh, and the spices give everything such a wonderful flavor."

Their waitress came over, introduced herself, and took their drink orders. She was a waif of a woman with huge breasts that were quite visible in her low-cut top. Emily wondered if they were hers or surgically enhanced. She watched Brody while he ordered. He never once looked down her shirt, even though his height offered him an eagle-eye view. Emily was pleasantly surprised. Most guys would have at least tried to sneak a peek. She might actually be in the company of a real live gentleman—although it didn't matter. He was definitely not her type, and he had lied on his profile by posting that picture and stating that he had an athletic build in the description. She wondered if that picture was of a family member who closely resembled him. She had lied a little too, but not like him. She merely posted an old picture that knocked a few years off her age.

The waitress quickly returned with their drinks. Neither one of them wanted an appetizer so they went ahead and placed their entrée selections and relinquished their menus. Brody still hadn't looked down the young lady's blouse. Instead, he looked at her. Emily took a sip of her water and noticed that Brody seemed to be studying her. It made her feel self-conscious. She began to squirm.

"Why are you staring at me?"

He smiled, showing those dimples again and then asked, "Let me ask you something. How long ago was that picture taken that you posted?"

Emily coughed and took another sip of her water. After she swallowed and cleared her throat she said, "What?"

"Don't get me wrong. You are still beautiful, but it's obvious that's what you used to look like. So, how old is the picture? C'mon, you can tell me." Emily began to turn red from embarrassment, but then Brody started laughing and soon Emily found herself laughing too. Although, she wasn't sure way.

"My picture was from 10 years ago before two kids, a divorce, and depression. I like that picture a lot, by the way. I was happy then, and life was really good. Not that my life isn't good now, but back then, it was *really* good."

"I feel you. And it's okay. As you can see," he said patting his stomach, "I posted an old picture too. That picture was five years ago before I had my car accident. It was bad, but I'm glad I had it because it was when they were checking for underlying damage that the doctors discovered that I had cancer. Thank God they caught it early, but I had to take steroids that made me blow up like a blimp. Believe it or not, I've actually lost weight. I was bummed about it for a while, but I'm taking control of my life again. I'm working out. Trying to eat healthier, and I'm even going on dates. For a while, I didn't want anyone to see me like this, and I didn't go anywhere."

Emily furrowed her brow. *This poor man*, she thought to herself. "I hate to hear that. I wondered what happened. Are you okay now?"

"Yep. I'm now cancer free. God is good."

"All the time," said Emily in response. "I hate you had to go through that, but I'm glad that you're all right. Life has a funny way of turning our world upside down. If someone had told me that my husband and I would ever separate, I would have told them that they were crazy. We were happy and in love for several years, and then we seemed to grow apart. What about you? What's your story?"

"I've never been married, but I did live with a woman for six years until I found out she was sleeping with another bodybuilder who went to the gym where we both worked out. I was actually headed to his house to beat the crap out of him when I had my accident. He got off easy, if you ask me, but he got his. My ex had a set of twins by him, and the child support payments are killing him," Brody laughed again, but Emily saw a hint of sadness in his eyes. He'd been through a lot. She didn't want to ruin the evening with such somber topics and decided to try to liven things up.

"What's your favorite movie?" she said.

"I love action. Anything with Jason Statham or The Rock in it gets my vote," he said.

Emily got excited. "I love action movies too. Jason is one of my favorites, but I also love martial arts. Bruce Lee, Jet Li, Jackie Chan, Michelle Yeoh, Chow Yun-Fat, or anybody else that kicks butt. *Kill Bill* is one of my favorites. I really wish they would make another sequel. Uma Thurman did her thing in those."

"Yeah, and who would have thought that Liam Neeson would become the world's oldest action hero," Brody chimed in.

"Yeah. It's like he picked up where Sean Connery left off," Emily laughed. Yes, Liam was a little up in age, but his movies were awesome. Emily thought he was sexy, and she loved his accent. However, he couldn't hold a candle to her beloved Denzel Washington.

Brody and Emily continued to talk of movies until the servers brought their food. It looked delicious. Brody prayed over the food, and they both dove in. Emily couldn't remember the last time she said grace. She used to, but one day she stopped, and it wasn't for any particular reason. It was nice that Brody initiated it. She needed to do it more often.

After a few bites, they resumed their conversation. The conversation was easy. It felt natural, as if she was talking to a friend she hadn't seen in a while. They both told stories about their families and their childhood. They even had a few things in common. They were both the middle child. They both enjoyed going to movies during the day when the theatres were less crowded. They both enjoyed Ben and Jerry's ice cream. His favorite was Peanut Butter Fudge™, and hers was Karamel Sutra™. They talked about their jobs and what they loved and what they hated about their chosen professions. Emily was a librarian at a local community college, and Brody did IT for the school system. He had a great sense of humor. He cracked jokes and made her laugh throughout the evening. She had to admit that she was having a really good time. She couldn't believe that she was about to let a funny, charming man with great conversation pass her by because he was larger than what she was used to. She no longer cared about how big he was. Brody was so much more than his size, and she was sure that with the proper diet, exercise, and the motivation she could provide, he could get back to the size he used to be. He may never be able to body-build like he used to because of some of the back injuries he sustained during his accident, but she was sure he could get smaller. Pam not showing up was a good thing because she would have surely used her as an excuse to leave right after the introductions.

After dinner, they split a large piece of warm chocolate cake topped with vanilla ice cream. By the time they finished, it was 9 p.m. Emily almost hated for the evening to end, but she knew it had to. The waitress brought the check, and Brody reached into pants pocket and pulled out a white piece of paper.

"What's that?" Emily said.

Brody waved his hand. "Oh, this is just a coupon I found online. I'm always trying to find ways to save money."

"That's totally something I would do. I'm an extreme couponer. I clip coupons for everything and save on everything and stockpile it. I've got 35 tubes of toothpaste and 26 packages of tissue in my basement," said Emily.

Brody laughed. "No wonder you have such nice teeth, and I'm sure your bum is really clean. I'm so glad that you're not one of those chicks who looks down on guys who use coupons. I saw this big debate about it on social media one day. I, myself, think that it's stupid and shallow for a woman to deduce that a man lacks class or is cheap because he uses a coupon."

"Oh really? Why?" said Emily.

"If a man uses a coupon, it allows him to spend more money on the evening. I'm not rich, but I enjoy a nice meal at a nice restaurant, and I like my guests to be able to do the same. Say, for instance, if this were the weekend instead of the weekday, I might ask you to join me for a stroll along the river walk and buy you a rose from one of the vendors. Maybe we'd go to a late movie afterward. Saving money on the meal allows me to be able to have more money to spend on the beautiful woman whose company I am enjoying. I may even be able to take her out more often."

Brody was looking at Emily and smiling. He had called her beautiful several times, but this time, her insides went warm. No one had called her that since her divorce. Actually, before the divorce. The waitress came by and took Brody's payment along with his coupon. Emily knew that she couldn't let this man get away. She had to make sure she could see him again.

"Brody, I had a really good time tonight. I feel like we have a connection. If you're up for it, I'd love to see you again," she said.

Brody smiled at Emily again. Those dimples were now beyond adorable, and she could imagine cradling his face in her hands as they kissed. Brody hesitated before he spoke. "I had a good time tonight too. This was fun, but I must confess. You're not really my type. Yes, you are beautiful, but you're a little bigger than I like my women. I also like women with large breasts. I mean yours are okay but did you see the rack on our waitress? I like you. I want to see you again, but dating you is going to be different for me."

Emily scoffed. She could not believe that the sumo wrestler of a man in front of her told her she was too big and her breasts were too small. She was like a size 18. If he were a woman, he would be a size 46! Furthermore, if he wanted to see some extra cleavage all he had to do was look down. His man boobs were at least a 34A.

Emily was about to cock a major attitude but instead she laughed! It was a hearty laugh that came from the pit of her stomach and then traveled all the way down to her toes. She had to be in some sitcom and not know it. What happened would have been hilariously funny if it had happened on her television screen, but it didn't. It was happening to her right then in real time. What were the odds that she and her date would both think the other was too big?

"What's so funny?" said Brody.

"I was thinking the exact same thing. I usually date smaller men but I've had such a good time that I don't care about your size. We've got too much in common to walk away because of aesthetics. Raise your water glass. I'd like to propose a toast."

Brody sat up tall in his seat and then raised his glass as instructed.

Emily raised her own glass and said, "To not dating your type. May opposites attract, preconceived notions be lost, and beautiful bonds be formed."

"Here, here" said Brody. "Maybe we could shed a few pounds together?"

Emily looked at the new teddy bear in her life and smiled. "If it's God's will," she said and then laughed again.

The Preacher and the Princess

A fool takes no pleasure in understanding, but only in expressing his opinion. — Proverbs 18:2

I do not date preachers, pastors, ministers, bishops, apostles, or whatever they are calling themselves these days. If he stands in the pulpit and has clergy on his car, I don't want him. I don't like sharing my man. Sharing a man with his job and his family is enough, but to have to share him with an entire church? No, thank you. The minute some female congregant calls my house in the middle of the night asking to speak to my husband I'm going to lay down my religion. I don't care if her husband just died. I need her to talk to Jesus until a decent hour and *then* call mine. He can't bring hers back. I might even ban holy oil because there won't be any laying of hands on other women going on during my watch. I am a princess, and my husband needs to be free to cater to me and my needs on a regular basis. At least that's what I told myself.

Then, I met Cyrus. Cyrus is unlike any pastor I've ever known. He's been married before and has two beautiful boys whom he shares custody of with his ex. I love watching him interact with them as well as my own son and daughter. They like him a lot. Whenever we're all together we feel like a family. Cyrus loves God and he loves ministry. He can preach too. Every Sunday, souls get saved, breakthroughs abound, and the Holy Ghost comes on in to move the people in a mighty way. The anointing on him is so strong, I think the man was bathed in the river of Jordan as an infant. But he takes the time to step away from the church and enjoy life. Most people are surprised when I tell them he also writes poetry and plays guitar. Some nights he even plays at a local club with a band. The first time I heard him sing "Still Waiting" by Prince in a beautiful falsetto, I knew he was one of a kind.

Cyrus is a good man, and I have thoroughly enjoyed our courtship. He makes sure that I know I'm special to him, and he tries to create a healthy balance between his family, his ministry, and his social life. There's only one thing that concerns me, or should I say *person.* That's Cyrus's supermodel-looking assistant, Essence. She's 25 with curves like a Hot Wheels track and flawless skin. I don't like her, and I don't trust her. The way she dotes on Cyrus is sickening. *"What do you need, Pastor?" "What can I get for you, Pastor?" "Can I get buck naked and dance for you, Pastor?"* Well, she probably doesn't go *that* far, but I bet she would if he let her. Cyrus assured me that I had nothing to worry about, but that chick has my temptress radar on high alert every time she comes around.

Cyrus asked me to meet him at our favorite restaurant this evening and wear something nice. We've been dating about eight months now, and I think he's going to propose. I made sure I was looking runway ready, but I don't think any amount of preparation could have equipped me for what was to come. The conversation went something like this.

Cyrus: Thank you for joining me tonight, Evelyn. You look lovely.

Me: Thank you, Cyrus. You look very handsome. I love when you wear black.

Cyrus: I know. That's why I wore it. I know you're wondering why I asked you here tonight. I wanted to talk to you about our relationship. I really enjoy spending time with you. It's been refreshing to be in the company of a woman who looks at me and sees Cyrus and not Pastor Wilkins. When I am with you, I can truly relax and be myself with no fear of judgment. I've been doing a lot of thinking about my future and what I want in a mate. I'd like for us to take our relationship to the next level and begin dating exclusively.

If you could have seen the look on my face! There I was, waiting for this fool to get down on one knee and place a ring on my finger—and he said something about dating exclusively!!!

Me: What does that mean?

Cyrus: That means that we will only see each other.

Me: I thought we were already exclusive. I left all of my other suitors alone a month after I met you. Didn't you?

Cyrus: Well, no. I kept seeing other women until I was sure you were the one.

Me: How many other women?

Cyrus: Why does that matter? A number isn't important. All that matters is that now you are my one and only.

Me: It is important to me. How many, Cyrus?

Cyrus: About three.

Me: You were seeing three other women? Wining and dining them like you do with me? Did you cuddle and kiss them like you do me? Did you take them around your children too? Did you sleep with any of them?

Cyrus: Don't be ridiculous. I was actually already seeing them when I met you, but the more I got to know you, the less time I wanted to spend with them. No, I didn't cut them off immediately. I had to make sure that you were the one I wanted to be with. For the last two months, any free time I had available has gone to you.

To answer your other questions, yes, one of them has met my children, but that's because she is a longtime friend of the family. And no, I'm not sleeping with anyone. When I told you I was practicing abstinence, I was telling the truth. I haven't had sex in years. Please don't get upset. They are my past, and you, Evelyn, are my present, and if we do this right, my future.

I sucked my teeth. So the preacher wants to be a player.

Me: Okay. If it's in the past, I can move on. So, does exclusive mean we are in a relationship?

Cyrus: No, not yet. It means that we aren't seeing other people.

Me: That sounds like a relationship to me, Cyrus.

Cyrus: It's one step before the relationship.

Me: So how long does it take to advance to a relationship?

Cyrus: I don't know. I'm not on any sort of schedule. You've got to understand that I can't afford to rush into anything with anyone. I have to be sure that the woman I bring into my life is the right woman for my boys and my congregation. I require complete loyalty and discretion. It is imperative that I take things slow. I must make sure that any woman I am with can easily maneuver the many facets of my life properly. Wife, stepmother, and first lady. You are of particular interest to me but also a great concern because you have never played any of those roles and will be thrust into all three simultaneously.

Me: I have no problems with taking things slow. I am sure you will find that I am well equipped to handle any role I am thrust into, as you say. However, I do have a problem with being made to think I was the only one, and I was not. I also have a problem with a man monopolizing all my time and asking me to disregard any other options without a commitment. In my opinion, we should just move forward with a relationship.

Cyrus: Darling, do you hear what I'm saying? I am giving up all other options as well. I want you to be the only woman in my life. I'm not ready for a relationship.

Me: Yeah, I heard you. I also heard 'I want to forgo the commitment in case I decide I want to go out with another woman.'

Cyrus: Maybe this was a mistake. Maybe we're not ready for this stage. I thought you, of all people, would understand. Especially since you don't usually date pastors. I thought you might like to gently ease into this as well. I haven't really included you in my church life, but since we've reached this level, I had plans to do so to allow you to truly see what you have to deal with.

Me: I disregarded my no-dating-pastors rule the moment I accepted your invitation to dinner. I believe I'd make a good first lady. Especially if it means I am your wife.

Cyrus: Good because whoever I am with still has to have a compassionate and giving spirit. She also must understand the rigors of being with a man of the cloth. I am not looking for someone to immerse herself in the church, but she does have to be understanding on the days that I must immerse myself.

I wondered why he was talking about me in third person. Out of the corner of my eye, I noticed a woman in a tight, red dress approaching our table. Cyrus noticed her too and stopped talking.

Woman: Pastor Wilkins, is that you? You prayed for me and my husband and our marriage during a conference last year. You have no idea how much that meant to us.

Me: Excuse me, ma'am, but don't you see us talking? What you just did was very rude. You didn't even say excuse me or acknowledge my presence. Mail him a note to the church or something. We are trying to discuss the future of our relationship here.

The woman opened her mouth and then grabbed her chest. I guess she was shocked because no sound came out of that gaping hole, even though I could clearly see all the fillings in her teeth. She was being overly dramatic, if you ask me.

Cyrus: Ha, ha, ha! Please don't mind her. We are in a private counseling session, but your intrusion is quite all right. I certainly remember you and your husband. I'm glad I could be of some service. How is he doing?

She was suddenly all smiles. Her fast recovery proved she was being dramatic.

Woman: He's doing well, and so are we as a couple. We decided to go to counseling and give our marriage one last good try, and it has worked in our favor.

Cyrus: I'm glad to hear that. I apologize that I can't chat longer, but this woman is very troubled. I fear she may do harm to herself or others. It is imperative that I get through to her.

I almost choked on the food in my mouth. Cyrus was insinuating that I was mentally ill.

Woman: I understand, Pastor. Let God use you. I'll add you both to my prayers.

Cyrus: Thank you. Give your husband my regards.

I waited until she was out of earshot before I spoke.

Me: What are you doing? Why would you tell a perfect stranger that?

Cyrus: If you can be ugly, I can too. What you did is exactly why I want to continue dating. I need to know that you can handle the interruptions that come with dating a pastor. What I do in some people's minds places me in celebrity status. Seeing me is almost like seeing Morris Chestnut.

Me: Morris? Really? I think that's taking it a bit too far. However, if we are dating exclusively, why wouldn't it be okay for me to let people know we are involved? I will not allow you to behave as if I'm some dirty little secret. Besides, she was being rude.

She didn't even say excuse me or acknowledge my presence when she walked up.

Cyrus: Of course you aren't a dirty secret, but that doesn't mean I want the world in our business either. Perhaps we should have this conversation in private. Why don't we table it until later? I don't want to ruin our romantic evening.

Me: Romantic? It's nice, but it's far from romantic. I'm not feeling turned on at all. In fact, I'm turned off. Are there any other things you need to tell me, Cyrus?

Cyrus: Well, there is one. If we are going to proceed, I have to be forthright and honest. My assistant and I had a moment of indiscretion two years ago. It only happened once, and I realized we made a mistake immediately after it happened. We both agreed to keep our attraction for each other at bay, and she has continued to work for me. I allowed her to remain as my assistant because she is very good at her job and a woman with her skill set and pleasant demeanor is hard to find.

Me: I knew it! I see the way she looks at you all goo-goo-eyed. And, 'by mistake,' do you mean that you slept with her?

Cyrus: Of course not. We merely kissed. It was hot and heavy kissing with heaving petting and some nudity, but I assure you that it went no further than that. As I stated, that was years ago. She's a girl, and I need a woman. It happened after the death of my mother. She was attempting to console me, and things went too far. I actually think she did it to see if she could. We talked about it afterward and both agreed it was wrong. We haven't even come close to doing anything like that again. She even has a boyfriend now. He attends the church. I assure you that was the only time, and it will never happen again.

I grabbed my purse and rose from my seat.

Me: Thank you for being honest. I know you didn't have to tell me, but this is a lot to digest in one sitting. Excuse me, but I need to go pee, powder my nose, and pray.

I really didn't need to do any of those things. Well, maybe I should have prayed, but instead, I gave myself a pep talk. I've been giving myself bathroom pep talks since I was four. Whenever my parents did something I didn't like, I would go in the bathroom and talk it out with myself. When I arrived at the ladies' room, I looked in all the stalls to make sure they were empty before I locked the bathroom door. I looked at myself eye to eye in the mirror.

I said, "Be rational about this, Evelyn. You cannot let the past ruin your future. You're no saint. You did way more than kiss someone you worked with back in the day. He's a good man. He treats you well, and he's trying to make you a permanent fixture in his life. No, this isn't the way you would have done it. It would have been nice to know that there were three other women in the picture, but you never asked if he was seeing anyone else. You merely assumed he wasn't. You know one of the primary rules is ask because men rarely volunteer that type of information. This 'dating exclusively' thing seems a little odd, though. Either two people are together, or they're not. But you can't deny that you want him all to yourself, and this is one step closer to having it. Actually, you do have him, but it's without the title. In the past, you've made the mistake of walking away simply because a man didn't say or do things the way you thought he should in the time you thought he should. Remember Darren, Paul, Elliott, and Warren? All Warren did was ask you to be patient until he finished dental school so his attention and his finances wouldn't have to be divided. But, noooo, you wanted a commitment right then. You told the man if he wasn't willing to sacrifice, he didn't really love you. Now he's making six figures and married to someone else. Evelyn, don't be so selfish and foolish again.

"You have to admit that you haven't felt this way about a man in a long time. It's obvious that he's smitten with you. He communicates with you every day, does little things to make you feel special, and takes you out on a regular basis. You owe it to yourself to see how far you two can take this thing before you call it quits simply because he isn't taking this at the pace you might like. Yes, it is uncomfortable that he kissed his assistant. They do spend a lot of time together, but get over it. He said there was nothing there. He said he wants a woman, and that woman is you. Cyrus has never given you a reason to doubt his truthfulness. She probably does still want him and is patiently waiting for another opportunity to take advantage of him again. Don't give her a reason to console him because you kicked the man to the curb. If you play your cards right, you can marry the good pastor and request that he fire her soon after the wedding. Don't rock the boat, Evelyn. This could be smooth sailing right into the love and the life you've always wanted. Patience and understanding, girl."

Someone banged on the bathroom door. I yelled, "Just a minute," and then used the bathroom, washed my hands, and freshened my makeup. As I exited, I held my head up high and walked back toward our table as if I was the baddest female in the place, because as far as I was concerned, I was. I gave the good pastor a pleasant smile and a full kiss on the lips. I really did want this man. I'd play by his rules for a little while and see where this was headed. Perhaps he was right. Maybe I did need time to learn if I could handle sharing him with the church, or anyone else, for that matter.

Me: Baby, I understand. We'll try it your way. I'd love to date you exclusively.

Pastor: Thank you for trusting me and giving us a fighting chance. I need to tell you something else, though. Evelyn, I'm scared. I think you are a magnificent woman, but I haven't been in a relationship since my divorce. I've only dated, and none of them were serious. I'm terrified of falling in love and having another woman leave me because she can't handle all the pressure that comes with being a pastor's wife. It wasn't all her fault. I made a lot of mistakes in my first marriage. I forgot that my first commitment was to my family. I put the church before my wife and spent too little time at home. I allowed other women in the church to disrespect and intimidate my wife by having easy accessibility to me because they held high-ranking positions within the church. I learned some valuable lessons, and I promise that when I do remarry, I will be a better husband.

Me: Cyrus, I don't expect a perfect man, because I'm not perfect. What I do expect is respect, honesty, and quality time. You have tried to show me that the entire time we've been dating, despite your busy life. Keep doing what you are doing and we should be fine. I have no intention of getting between you and the work God has given you to do. I've seen your gift in action and the blessing you are to others. The people need you, and I know it. Yet, you are still human, and you can't do it all. When you are weary, let me be your refuge, your confidante, your quiet place of peace. I can be that cool pool of refreshing water you dip your aching body in to find rejuvenation, if you let me. I want to be a blessing to you, your boys, and your church.

Cyrus: Thank you, Evelyn. I really needed that reassurance. I promise I'll make this journey with me worth your while.

Me: You better, 'cause if you don't, I'm going to tell the entire congregation you played tonsil hockey with your 25-year-old secretary. Really, Cyrus, you're almost old enough to be her father.

Cyrus: You're kidding, right?

Me: Let's table that discussion for later. I'd hate to ruin this romantic dinner.

We both laughed. Mine was that evil laugh that villains give in Disney animated movies. His was a nervous *this woman might actually be crazy* laugh. He has no idea. Let the exclusivity begin. We'll see if this preacher can handle this princess.

What Goes Around Comes Around

Do nothing out of selfish ambition or vain conceit, but in humility consider others better than yourselves. Each of you should look not only to your own interests, but also to the interests of others. Your attitude should be the same as that of Christ Jesus.
— Philippians 2:3-5

Alayna looked at her phone, rolled her eyes, and then looked over at her mother. "In what alternate universe is it okay for a man to text you all day instead of call and use high school shorthand text talk when he does? Malik and I have been dating for three months, but I don't think this is going to work. I keep feeling like I settled," she said.

Her mother turned her body toward her and then cocked her head to the side. "Settled? Darling, what do you mean?"

"I'm a successful executive assistant at a Fortune 500 company. I have a degree. He crawls around in people's attics and in their backyards, fixing their heaters and air conditioners. You taught me to use correct English. He really believes that 'be' is a verb. It's embarrassing sometimes."

"Young lady, when did you get so high and mighty? Did you forget that your father gets dirty for a living? He is a mechanic, and he makes good money too. If it wasn't for him, you wouldn't have your fancy degree. He sent you and both your brothers to college. How dare you look down on a man just because he works with his hands! Do you know how much he makes? Last I checked, it cost a minimum of $40 for someone to show up and look at your air conditioner. That's not a bad fee just for pulling up in someone's driveway."

Alayna took a deep breath. "He makes a decent amount of money, Mother, but that's not my point. I want someone more refined. Someone who doesn't come home with dirt under his fingernails every night. Someone who does more than drink beer and watch sports. Malik is a good man, but he's a simple man. I believe a woman should date a man who is above her social status, not below. I need more."

She pulled her BMW into the corner gas station and parked next to pump one. Alayna spent the day with her mother. She took her to her doctor's appointment, and then they had a late lunch at Evergreen Grill. They both tried their famous lobster burger. It was so big they were unable to eat it all and took the remainder with them. The day had been pleasant; she really didn't want to ruin it with a lecture from her mother. She should have known better than to bring up her love life to a woman who had been married to the same man since she was 18. What did she know about dating?

Candace Kincaid looked at her only daughter and thought to herself, *What am I going to do with this woman-child? My husband spoiled this girl rotten, and now some poor man will have to deal with the monster he created. She thinks she's too good for her own good.* "I wondered why my daughter was 35 years old and still single. Now I know. Your standards are too high, young lady. If you were all that, you'd be married by now. Last I checked, you couldn't cook, and you are a terrible homemaker. You think you know everything, and this year alone, I bet you've gained an additional 50 pounds. You need to take some self-inventory and be happy that a good man like Malik even looked your way. That degree doesn't make you better than anybody else, and Malik's lack of one doesn't make him inferior. When it comes to men, what you need is a God-fearing man who loves the Lord, doesn't mind working hard for what he wants, and has a good heart. That man adores you. What did his text say?"

Alayna was fuming. She didn't understand what her lack of culinary skills or her weight had to do with any of this. She had plenty of girlfriends around her age who were still single. Yes, she had gained a few pounds, but so what? She still looked good every time she left her house. This was about class, and Malik was mannerable enough, but he lacked class. She probably never would have even looked at him, but when he came over to fix her air conditioner, her date for the evening had cancelled. He gave her a horrible excuse about his car insurance lapsing, and he didn't want to drive his car, and he didn't like riding in other people's cars, blah, blah, blah. Malik noticed something was wrong and asked if he could take her out after his shift "to put a smile on your face." They went to dinner and had a great time. Malik was good company, but she never meant to get serious about him. He was just supposed to be someone to go out with until someone better came along, but somehow, they ended up becoming more. She liked him a lot but wasn't sure if she could see herself sharing a lifetime with him. He was so rough around the edges.

"I asked you a question, Alayna," said her mother.

"It said he was thinking of me, and he hoped I was having a good day," Alayna replied through clenched teeth.

"That's sweet. No, it wasn't a phone call, but at least he let you know that you were foremost in his thoughts. What's wrong with that?"

"Nothing, Mother. You are absolutely right." She knew this conversation was not going to end in her favor, no matter what she said, so she might as well agree.

Alayna exited the car to pump her gas. She wished she didn't have to get back in because she had no desire to continue that conversation. Her mother didn't understand. Yes, her father was a mechanic, but he was also well-rounded. He actually came from a middle-class family himself, but because he had an affinity for cars, he chose to be a mechanic. Grandfather actually wanted him to be an accountant. Besides, her father wasn't merely a mechanic. He was the owner of a very successful repair shop for luxury cars. He hadn't gotten his hands dirty in years. He paid people to dirty theirs.

Alayna thought about going inside the gas station to pay for her gas so that she could avoid her mother a little longer but decided against it. It was hot outside. It wasn't exactly a short walk to get inside, and she was wearing six-inch stilettos. It would be in her best interest to take advantage of modern conveniences. She slid her debit card into the machine located on the pump and followed the prompts that told her to put in her pin number.

A voice behind her said, "Excuse me. I hate to see a woman as beautiful as you pumping her own gas. Would you do me the honor of allowing me to do it?"

She was slightly startled and turned around to find standing there a gentleman with golden brown skin, a close-shaven head, and a goatee smiling at her. The sparkle of his smile seem to rival that of his brown eyes.

Although the gleam coming from the expensive Movado watch he wore had them both beat. Alayna smiled at him and then peered over his shoulder to the Jaguar he must have abandoned to come talk to her. She was familiar with that car. She actually test-drove one before she purchased her BMW. That was an $80,000 car, which was exactly why she left it sitting on the showroom floor.

"Are you sure you want to get your hands dirty pumping my gas? I mean, you look so nice in your suit."

"I wouldn't be a gentleman if I let you do it." He extended his hand. "By the way, I'm Lucius."

Alayna extended her hand in return. "I'm Alayna, and since you put it that way, far be from me to prevent you from fulfilling your gentlemanly duties. Pump away, sir."

"Alayna. A lovely name for a lovely woman," he said, then stepped closer to her and grabbed the 93 octane pump that was located to her left. Alayna could smell his cologne. It made her want to come closer and breathe it—and him—in more deeply. Lucius was nicely dressed in grey pants and a pink dress shirt which fit snugly to reveal a muscular build. It was obvious he took great pride in his appearance. His hands were nicely manicured, and his freshly shined shoes shone brightly in the sun. He was definitely a man who knew the importance of details. She wondered what he did.

"Thank you for your kindness, Lucius. Did you have a good day at work? I hope they didn't work you too hard."

He smiled. "It has been a productive day. As a principal of a successful brokerage firm, every day is critical. People trust me with their money, and I don't want to let them down."

"I'm sure you don't." *Handsome, a great dresser, and successful . . . Niiice*, she thought to herself.

"Alayna, I hope I'm not being too forward, but you are breathtaking. If you don't mind, I would like to get to know you better. Would you happen to be available for dinner tonight?"

She bit her bottom lip. She and Malik were dating but technically, Malik wasn't her man, so if she went out with Lucius, she wasn't actually cheating. Besides, this man had class oozing out of his pours. The very thing she felt her current love interest was badly in need of.

"I would love to," she said.

"Wonderful." Lucius finished pumping her gas and then reached into his pocket. "Here is my card. Please call my office shortly and leave your number on the voice mail. My assistant will call you with the details. Do you mind meeting me at the restaurant? I have a couple of meetings to attend before I conclude my workday, but I know I'll be famished when it's over. Also, I don't want to keep you out too late."

"Sure. I don't mind at all. I look forward to hearing from your . . . um . . . assistant." That was a first. No one had ever asked her to schedule a date with their assistant. Maybe a meeting, but not a date. Alayna got back in the car and put the card in her purse.

Her mother watched her with a look of interest. "Did I hear you accept an invitation to dine with that gentleman? I know it's none of my business, but aren't you dating Malik? How would you like it if he accepted a dinner invitation from another woman?"

Alayna took a deep breath before turning her head to address her mother. At 63 years old, her mother looked stunning. She was aging gracefully and could easily be featured in one of those magazine profiles of women who don't look their age. Alayna loved her mother, and she had no doubt that she loved her and only wanted the best for her, but she had to be one of the nosiest people on the planet. She never felt out of place interjecting in any of her children's lives, and since Alayna was the only girl, she seemed to get a double dose of unsolicited advice.

Alayna cranked up her car and reached her hand toward the knobs on her radio. "You're right, Mother," she said. "It's none of your business." She then turned the volume up and let the music flow loudly through her speakers. She and her mother drove the rest of the way in silence. Although her feelings were hurt, her mother took the hint. She did not like when her daughter shut her out, and she knew if she continued to question Alayna about her behavior, that was exactly what would happen.

The next day, Alayna came to work with a great big grin on her face. Her dinner with Lucius was divine. After calling his office, his assistance called her back with their dinner reservations for Folk's Folly, one of the premier steak houses in Memphis. Lucius arrived 30 minutes late, but when he did appear, it was with a rose and a heartfelt apology. He explained that one of his meetings took longer than he anticipated. During dinner, the conversation was lighthearted. They discussed classical music, politics, and current events. The most interesting part was discussing the plight of the African American male and the spree of recent killings of them by law enforcement officers. The chemistry between them was undeniable. Lucius knew how to use those sexy eyes to sear a pathway into her soul, and when he smiled at her, her internal thermometer skyrocketed to heat advisory proportions. She painstakingly tried not to fawn over him all evening, but it was hard for her not to wonder if those lips were as soft as they looked and what his chiseled chest would feel like pressed against her body. At the end of the evening, Lucius gave her sweet kiss on the lips, and his lips felt softer than she imagined. They exchanged cell phone numbers and agreed to meet again soon.

While she sat at her desk reminiscing about their date, her phone chimed, indicating that she had a text message

GUD MORN, BU T FUL. I MISS U.

She really did wish Malik would stop texting like he was a teenager. It irritated her to no end. She simply responded. THANKS. Five minutes later another text arrived.

I REALLY ENJOYED OUR TIME LAST NIGHT. THE BEAUTY OF THE ROSE I GAVE YOU PALED IN COMPARISON TO YOURS AND THE FRAGRANCE YOU WORE WAS EVEN MORE SWEET. I LOOK FORWARD TO SPENDING MORE TIME WITH YOU SOON. HAVE A GOOD AND PRODUCTIVE DAY, MY SWEET. LC

Alayna thought to herself, *Now that's how a grown man with a profession sends a text message.* Malik was a nice guy, but he was definitely no Lucius Cain.

Alayna and Lucius continued to see each other. She greatly enjoyed his company, although his busy work schedule caused him to have to reschedule their dates a couple of times, and he was always late. He often texted and took business calls during their outings, but she understood that he had a business to run. He took her to fancy restaurants, sent roses to her job, and showered her with compliments. He knew how to make a woman feel special. He always looked immaculate, and they made a cute couple. She could definitely see herself sharing a lifetime with him.

She hadn't seen Malik in a couple of weeks and often avoided his phone calls. He was starting to get suspicious, and Alayna knew that she had to end things with him. It wasn't fair to him or her. He was a good man, and he deserved to be with someone who could appreciate him, and she deserved to be with a man like Lucius. She asked him over for dinner at her apartment that evening. Malik showed up on time, like he always did. If he said he was going to be there at 7 p.m., he was there at 7 p.m. or earlier, and if he was late, there was a very good reason. He came over straight from work and was still in his uniform. He smelled of sweat and hard work. His blue pants and shirt with his name on it were covered in filth, indicating that he had to crawl under someone's home that day. He usually had to do that with older homes, but Alayna hated when he came over to her house looking disheveled. He put his work boots and uniform in the laundry room before taking a quick shower and changing into one of several outfits he kept at her place. This time, it was a wife beater, a pair of basketball shorts, and his do-rag.

Malik was an attractive man, but it was a different kind of attractiveness than Lucius. Malik was more urban. He had a homeboy look about him that put you in the mind of the men she saw in hip-hop videos. He was a product of the hood and had no desire to shed any of the habits he picked up over the years. She hated that he didn't think it was inappropriate to wear his do-rag out in public, and because of the work he did, his nails were always dirty. He started scrubbing them with a brush like she suggested, but no matter how hard he scrubbed, they always still held a small amount of dirt. He refused to get a professional manicure. He said a real man's hands looked like he did real work.

After his shower, Malik came into the kitchen, grabbed her and placed a kiss on her cheek. "Why you be in here frontin' like you cooking? Whatever you have smells good, but I know you ordered it. Come here, baby. I missed you." He began planting soft kisses on her neck. "I can tell you've picked up a couple of pounds, but I like my women thick. Maybe I'll add *you* to the menu."

Alayna's knees suddenly grew weak, and her body warm. Malik had several areas in which he could improve, but his lovemaking skills weren't one of them. He was sensuous and attentive. He always took his time and made sure that she enjoyed herself. He described himself as a pleaser and wasn't happy unless his woman was satisfied. He always held her afterward and stayed until the next morning. He wasn't a "wham bam thank you ma'am" kind of guy. His lips worked their way to her face and then kissed her mouth deeply. Alayna knew she had to stop this so she could do what she had to do. She wanted to take things to the next phase with Lucius, but she believed in closing one door before opening another. Lucius asked her about intimacy on their last date. She politely avoided it by telling him she wasn't ready yet. He said he understood. Alayna wanted to, but she wasn't the type of woman to sleep with two men.

She squirmed away from Malik's grasp. "I want to see other people," she said quickly. That wasn't the tactful way she rehearsed it, but she couldn't take the words back once they escaped her lips.

"Huh? What? Why? I thought we was happy. I'm happy," he said.

Alayna took another step back. "We were happy enough, but I don't think we're on the same level."

Malik gave her a puzzled look. "Level? What level is that? Baby, we good together, and you know it. I love you, girl."

"Malik, you can't possibly love me. We've only been dating four months."

"I've loved you since a month after we met. I thought you loved me too. You be spending all your time with me. You be making good love to me. I thought you wanted a future with me."

"I thought I did too, but after thinking it over, I don't think we're right for each other." Her gaze went slightly downward. She couldn't look him in the face. She then said softly, "I've met someone."

Malik's jaw grew hard, and Alayna saw the pectorals beneath his wife beater tighten. "I had my suspicions there was somebody else, but I didn't want to believe that you was the type of woman that would creep. I guess I was wrong. I thought we was together."

Alayna knew she had to explain this delicately. She had seen Malik mad once when a man spoke rudely to her at a convenience store. It wasn't a pretty sight.

"Malik, we were dating. We weren't in a relationship. It wasn't like we couldn't see other people. We just didn't. At least, not at first."

Malik slammed his fist on the table. "Do you have any idea how many women approach me each day? In the store, at church, on the job. I went to one home last week, and when I come back in the house after running to my truck, the owner was buck naked and offered to give me my money and a *special* tip. She was fine too. I turned her down. You wanna know why? Because all I be thinkin' 'bout is you and how these other women don't even compare to the woman in my life, so I ain't gon' waste my time. I'm being faithful, and you been going out with someone else. You concerned about levels when you know I make every bit as much as you do. You is a glorified sec-rah-tary—not a doctor or lawyer. Did you sleep with him?"

Alayna didn't like the way he made fun of her occupation, but she wanted him gone with as little drama as possible. "No," she said is a soft voice. " And this isn't about money."

"But you want to."

She didn't answer, but she didn't have to. Her eyes betrayed her, but so did Malik's. He looked her squarely in the face. She saw pain. She knew this would hurt him, but she had no idea he would react like this.

"I love you, woman, but I never stay where I'm not wanted. And for what it's worth, I don't *want* to see other people. It's all or nothing, and you already made your choice. For your sake, I hope this dude is everything you're looking for, because I'm a good man, and I know it. I may not be a part of the city's elite. I don't wear a suit every day, go to symphonies, or wine tastings. I ain't been to school to learn a bunch of stuff in books I probably won't remember, but I know how to love and take care of my woman. I was thinking 'bout put a ring on your finger and spending the rest of my days making you happy."

"I'm sorry, Malik. I never meant to hurt you," said Alayna. She tried to touch him, but he moved out of her reach and walked off.

Alayna sat down at the kitchen table while Malik went around her house, collecting his things, and then left. She felt bad about hurting him, but she truly felt that it had to be done if she was going to have any kind of future with Lucius.

The next week, Lucius invited her to his flawlessly decorated home on the grounds of a golf course for a romantic dinner. He cooked lobster tails with baked potatoes topped with sour cream and chives and steamed broccoli. There was plenty of champagne, and afterward, he fed her cheesecake before they attempted to watch a movie. It was hard because Lucius was feeling playful and continuously kissed and fondled her. She didn't mind, though. Alayna wanted him as badly as he wanted her. Before the movie ended, he grabbed her by the hand and took her to his bedroom to make love. However, it was not the sensuous experience she fantasized about. Lucius was rough and selfish and didn't seem to have an understanding of the importance of foreplay. He yanked her clothes off in haste and broke the zipper on her skirt. Instead of caressing her delicate skin, he pawed at her flesh. His kisses were quick and lacked passion. He kept licking her face as if he were a dog, and that was the *only* place he licked. He didn't seem to care if she enjoyed their moment as long as he climaxed. Which he did, quickly. Afterward, Lucius rolled over with his back toward her and went to sleep. Although she was in his bed right next to him, Alayna somehow felt incredibly alone. She looked over at him snoring loudly, and he no longer seemed charming or handsome. She wrapped her arms around herself and drifted off to sleep.

About an hour later, she was rudely awakened by Lucius. He asked her to leave because he had to rise early and needed to get a good night's rest. He said it was hard for him to sleep with someone else in his bed. He apologized but asked her to please be understanding and said he was looking forward to spending more time with her tomorrow. The Chamber of Commerce was having their annual awards dinner, and she was his date. Alayna obliged his request and left. She didn't quite know how to feel, but she knew she didn't feel good, wanted, or appreciated. Before she left, he said, "Sweetheart, you were great tonight." She wished she could say the same. That was the first time in her life that a man had made love to her—and then asked her to leave. She tried not to take it personally and instead focused on the fact that she was going to the awards dinner on the arm of Lucius Cain. It was a big deal among the business community, and all of the top business leaders and politicians would be there. She hoped they would have a good evening because this one ended horribly.

The next day, Alayna worked very hard to get all her tasks at work completed quickly so she could leave early and go get her hair done. After she left the salon, she stopped by the mall and let one of the makeup artists at the various counters do her face. Once she arrived home, she washed up and changed into a black dress with a plunging neckline and pearls. She had full perky breasts and the dress displayed them well. She chose a white beaded clutch and black, open-toed shoes with white beaded heels to complement her pearls. Alayna paused in front of her full-length mirror and was really pleased with her appearance, and she knew Lucius would be pleased too.

Later, Lucius arrived in the limo he rented for the evening, late as usual. When she opened the door he took her breath away in a tailored black tuxedo with an ascot instead of a bow tie. She smiled and then leaned in for a kiss, but Lucius's lips were stiff and cold, and his expression was even colder. His eyes traveled from her head to her toes disapprovingly. She spent her entire afternoon getting dolled up for him, but instead of appreciating her efforts, he scolded her for not wearing something more elegant and said next time, he would pick out her dress.

"Your hair looks nice. I prefer less makeup, though. You look like you should be climbing into a casket with all that foundation, but you will have to do because I don't have time to take you shopping. Now, shall we?"

He then headed to the car with an expectation for her to follow. Wasn't he supposed to escort her to the car? Alayna locked her door and walked to the limo. She felt like a child who had her balloon popped by the neighborhood bully. Lucius continued to critique her ensemble during the drive. She pretended to ignore him by looking out the window at the passing scenery.

Once they arrived at the Peabody Hotel, where the awards banquet was being held, they quickly entered the building and were shown to their seats. Lucius spent most of the evening talking to the other businessmen at the table instead of her. She recognized some of them from articles that appeared in the local newspaper, but she didn't know most of their names. Lucius didn't bother to even introduce her. She was forced to make idle chitchat with the other women at the table. Alayna was not used to such behavior. Whenever she and Malik went out, he treated her as if she was the only person in the room. She tried her best to enjoy the evening in spite of Lucius's rude behavior, but how could she? The room was decorated beautifully, the food was delicious, and the awards ceremony was well orchestrated, but Alayna was unhappy. Why was Lucius being so rude? Was her outfit so dreadful that he felt the need to punish her? The evening eventually ended, and Alayna decided to address his behavior when they were back in the limo. Lucius was not sympathetic.

"Do you know why I go to these events? To scout out new business. I cannot do that if I am babysitting you. If you are going to be with me, your job at these events is to sit there, look pretty, and win over their wives. Dates are for one-on-one attention, not business functions. They are about expanding my clientele, so I can make some more money to buy you a more suitable dress. I also need to get you a personal trainer. I never said anything before, but your behind is a little too fat for my taste. Luckily, we can do something about that. I've taken the liberty of making your first fitness appointment. It's at 10 a.m. Sunday. Her name is Brandy, and my assistant says she is fabulous. She helped her lose her baby weight after giving birth to twins. There was no way I was going to have a whale sitting at a desk in my front office." And then Lucius laughed as if he had said the most hilarious joke ever told.

Alayna was appalled. How dare he be so bold? She attended church on Sundays, and Lucius knew that. She wished she was bolder at that moment. She knew he needed to be set straight, but she didn't possess the courage or the words to do it. Malik would never have talked to her like that.

"Are you spending the night at my house tonight?" he asked as if everything was fine between them.

"No, I have a headache and work tomorrow. I need to go home and rest," she said.

"I figured as much. You women can be so sensitive. Remember, Alayna, a man like me is a hot commodity. Whatever you won't do, I guarantee you several other women will. I chose you because I see great potential in you. You complement me well. Please don't make me regret my decision.

"The night is still young. I think I'll stay out for a bit. My driver can take you home. Driver, please take me to the Westin. I believe they have live jazz tonight." The Westin hotel was about 5 minutes away. When they arrived, Lucius exited the car with a curt "good night" and a kiss on her cheek.

The drive to Alayna's home seemed longer than usual. Malik would have never sent her home alone. If she didn't feel well, he took her home and personally and tucked her in bed after getting her two Advil and some juice. He wouldn't let her do anything but rest. If it were biologically possibly, he would have emptied her bladder to prevent her from leaving her bed. The next morning when she awoke, he'd still be there to make sure she was feeling better and to fix her breakfast. What had she gotten herself into? The only person Lucius seemed to care about was himself.

Alayna didn't sleep well. She tossed and turned all night and woke up in the morning with a headache that was worse than the one she pretended to have the night before. She normally took time each morning to read her

Bible and pray. She didn't feel like doing it this morning, but the words of her mother rang in her head. "What if God decided not to wake you up because He didn't feel like it? You better give God some time."

She reached for her Bible on her nightstand where she kept it, and it fell open to Proverbs, chapter three. Her eyes drifted to verse five.

Trust in the Lord with all your heart and lean not on your own understanding; in all your ways submit to him, and he will make your paths straight.

Alayna immediately realized the error of her ways. She did not consult her Heavenly Father before dating Malik or Lucius. In a matter of months, she had been intimate with two men, and neither of them were her husband. She began to pray and ask God to direct her steps. She wanted a relationship, but more than anything, she wanted to please God. After her prayer, Alayna's headache was gone. She proceeded to get ready for work.

******

"C'mon, go!" Alayna screamed at the cars in front of her. I-40 was exceptionally busy that morning. There had been two wrecks, and one was quite serious. She had already passed the minor one and was now attempting to approach the second. As she sat impatiently in traffic, she noticed that there was smoke coming from the hood of her car. Alayna tried to maneuver over to the emergency lane to see what the problem was, but before she was able to cross one lane, her car stopped. She found herself sitting in the middle of the interstate. She turned on her flashers, then got out her phone and called Lucius. She would have called her father, but he was out of town. Besides, she wanted the man in her life at times like this. Lucius answered on the second ring. He sounded a little too happy for her taste. She quickly explained her predicament.

"Sorry, baby, but I have two very important meetings this morning. You're going to have to handle this yourself. I'm sure you have roadside assistance with your insurance. Have them come tow your car to the dealership and then get a loner car or take a cab to work. My 8 a.m. is here. Gotta go. I'll call and check on you later," he said and hung up. Alayna was almost sure she heard a woman laugh in the background. She immediately dialed his office and his assistant Christina answered. The two of them had developed a very friendly rapport since she began dating Lucius. She seemed a little more chipper than usual too.

"Oh, good morning, Alayna. How are you?" she asked in a singsongy voice.

"I'm fine, Christina. I wanted to call and tell you thank you for giving Lucius the name and number of your personal trainer. I'm looking forward to meeting Brandy on Sunday," she lied.

"Oh, it was my pleasure. She's a beast and will produce results. You may hate her when she's done, but I guarantee that you'll love the way you look."

"I have no doubt, honey. Listen, I'm trying to get in touch with Lucius. My car stopped on me. Can you put me through to him?"

"Oh, he's not here. He said he'd be working from home because he wasn't feeling well. By the way, I thought you looked lovely last night at the banquet. You and the boss man make a handsome couple, if I do say so myself. I can try to reach him for you and tell him about your dilemma," she sang.

"Thank you, Christina, but don't worry about disturbing him if he's not feeling well. I'll just handle it myself."

Alayna was determined to get to the bottom of this. She could not stand a liar. She used her cell phone to look up the number to the Westin and asked to be connected to Lucius Cain's room. He answered on the third ring.

"I am stuck in the middle of the interstate with a smoking car, and you are holed up in a hotel room with another woman. I thought you had class, but I see that you are a despicable, selfish man. We are through. Don't call me. Don't text me. I'd rather be single than with a snake like you."

Lucius tried to disguise his voice with a horrible English accent. "I'm sorry, ma'am, but I believe you have the wrong number. There is no one here but me and my lovely wife. Have a g'day, love, and I hope you find the bloke who is cheating on you." Then he hung up.

Tears stung Alayna's eyes. How could she have been so stupid? She let a good man like Malik go for a dog in tailor-made clothing. But this wasn't the time to cry. She had to handle her business at hand. Alayna called her father's auto repair shop, and the assistant manager said he would send someone to get her. She didn't have a problem waiting for the tow, but she did have a problem with sitting in her car in the middle of morning rush-hour traffic. It was starting to move a little more swiftly. She really did need to get it over to the side of the road, but she couldn't do it by herself.

Alayna got out of her car and tried to flag down a Good Samaritan. Someone did pull over . . . and she had never been so happy to see Malik in all her life. Her joy was short-lived when she realized that there was a woman in the car she didn't recognize. She assumed that was her replacement. As soon as the car stopped, he got out, maneuvered through traffic, and gave her a hug. She felt so safe when she was in his arms. She eagerly pressed her body against his and snuggled her face in his shoulder. She probably shouldn't have held on to him so long with his woman in the car, but she didn't care. She really needed that hug.

"Are you OK, baby?" he whispered in her ear.

"I'm fine now that you're here. I don't know what happened, but my car starting smoking, and then it cut off. A tow truck is on the way, but I don't feel safe sitting here in the middle of traffic."

"It's not safe—for you or your car. Someone who isn't paying attention could run right into you. Let's get you both to the side of the road." He waved over to the car, and a beautiful woman with a walk that could almost stop traffic got out and headed toward them. Several people in passing cars turned their heads to look at her. She approached them with a less-than-pleased expression.

"Sam, this is Alayna." He offered no more of an explanation than that. The two women eyed each other up and down and said hello. "I need you to help me get her car to the side of the road. Sam, you direct traffic around us. Alayna, you put the car in neutral and steer, and I'll push." Sam did as she was told and diverted oncoming cars to go around them while the two of them maneuvered the car from the middle lane to the emergency lane.

Once they were safely on the side of the road, Malik told Alayna to get in the car with Sam and she would take her to work. He would wait on the tow truck and get her car to the shop.

Alayna shook her head. "Thanks, but no thanks. Being in the car with your new woman is a little too awkward for me."

Malik laughed. "My woman? Do you think I could replace you so easily and quickly? I'm not like you, Alayna. When I'm in love with one woman I can't just go get with another one. I need time to myself. Sam is the office assistant at my job. She was giving me a ride to work because my car is down too."

Alayna thought about Lucius's betrayal and began to cry. "I'm sorry. Breaking up with you was the stupidest thing I've ever done. You were good to me. You were faithful to me. Can you forgive me?"

Malik's face held no emotion when he responded, but his voice held a little warmth. "It's a mistake you're going to have to live with because I don't trust you now. I'm helping you because I care what happens to you, but we will never be the same."

Alayna wiped her tears with her hand. She had to accept the consequences of her actions and take the lesson life was dealing her. "I understand and thank you. You are a great guy, and you deserve someone a lot better than me. But if it's all the same to you, I'll wait on the tow-truck driver. I've interrupted enough of your day. You're already late for work."

"No, Alayna. You can be so stubborn. I am not leaving you on the side of the road. Now get in the car!"

"I'll be fine. I'm a big girl." Before she knew it, Malik grabbed her face with both hands and kissed her. His thick, juicy lips felt like heaven against hers. His tongue entered her mouth and began a passionate dance with hers. She was fully aware that they were on the side of the interstate and anyone could see them, but she didn't care. She missed having a man kiss her like he desired her. He suddenly broke away and said. "Why do you have to be so pigheaded? My God, you look beautiful. I always loved this outfit on you. If we weren't on the side of the road I'd make love to you right here. I miss you so much, Alayna."

With a teary face, smeared makeup, and sweaty clothes, this man thought she was beautiful and wanted to make love to her. Last night while dressed in some of her finest attire, another man made her feel like she had a hunchback and three eyes and then left her so he could be with another woman. She made the mistake of thinking things would be better with someone else other than Malik because he wasn't on her level. Instead, Malik was a better person than she would ever be.

"I miss you too, Malik. I didn't realize how much I loved you or how wonderful you are until I pushed you away. Please give me another chance. Could you please try to forgive me? You're the man I want. You're all the man I need." Alayna hoped her pleading would penetrate the tough exterior he was trying to erect.

Malik looked up at the vehicle approaching them and let her go. "Your wrecker is here. Please go get in the car with Sam. She'll take you where you need to go. I'll call you after it's safely at your father's shop. We'll talk later. This isn't the time or the place."

This time, Alayna didn't put up a fight. She wasn't in a position to be defiant or make demands. The ball was in Malik's court, and she had to wait and see what kind of play he chose to make. She hoped he could forgive her and come back into her life, but only time would tell.

She thanked him, and then the two of them walked over to Sam's Chrysler 300. He said a few words to Sam and then opened the door for Alayna to get in. Judging from the stank look Sam gave her, it was obvious Malik had confided in her what happened between the two of them.

"Where to?" she said with an attitude.

Alayna gave Sam her parents' address. She was a sweaty mess and needed to shower and change clothes before going to the office. She had clothes at her parents' house, and she could use her father's car while he was out of town. Besides, she didn't like the look on Sam's face and thought it best that she didn't know where she lived or worked.

"Thank you for doing this," said Alayna.

"Thank Malik. If it was up to me, you'd still be in the middle of traffic trying to flag down some help. Malik is a good guy. You hurt him bad."

"I know. I was stupid."

"Yep. You're all he ever talked about. And now that I see you, I don't see what he was so excited about. You ain't all that." She looked at Alayna and rolled her eyes.

"I guess I deserve that," said Alayna and sniffed. "I'm sure you feel he could do much better with you?"

Sam sucked her teeth. "Naw. We're not like that, but I do care about him. I don't like what you did one bit." She reached into the glove compartment, pulled out some napkins and handed them to Alayna.

"Thank you. I want him back, but he says he no longer wants me," said Alayna

"That's BS. He's just hurt is all. Show him you're sincere and he'll take you back. Give him some time, but you've got to accept a man like him as he is. Education doesn't make you loyal, kindhearted, or loving. You can't get that at school. A man like that will love you with everything he's got until the day he dies, but you've got to be willing to do the same for him. If not, leave him alone. Because if he takes you back and you hurt him again, you will have to deal with me *and* my friend named Nina," said Sam.

Alayna knew that Nina was a nickname for a nine millimeter gun. She didn't like being threatened, but she was in no mood to fight. Besides, Sam was right. The kind of class Malik had wasn't taught in charm school. "I understand," was all she said.

Alayna swore to herself that she would get Malik back if it was the last thing she did. Her mother was right, and so was Sam. She wasn't all that, but Malik was, and the next time they were together she was going to show him. As for Mr. Lucius Cain, she never wanted to see him again!

Do the Right Thing

A beautiful woman who lacks discretion is like a gold ring in a pig's snout. — Proverbs 11:22

Is it a criiiiime . . .

Jennifer sat in the dark listening to her favorite songstress, Sade, belt out a song that was doing little to ease her conflicted mind. The wail of the saxophone substituted for the cries she wouldn't allow to escape her ruby-colored lips. The contents of the bottle she held by the neck with her right hand offered little solace as well. She sat enveloped in the pitch-black darkness of her apartment as if she was in hiding. The only illumination came from the buildings that made up the Nashville skyline that were visible through the large windows of her luxury 10th-floor apartment. The dark cloak caused by nightfall usually gave her some peace, but not tonight. She tried her best to dismiss the thought of him. Him, being Felix, but he wouldn't be done away with so easily. Jennifer took a long swig of her Moscato. The liquid felt cool as it traveled downward, coating her throat. She pressed the bottle to her face to allow her to experience its coolness outwardly as well. It wasn't hot tonight, and she wasn't sick, but she felt as if she had a fever. She wasn't much of a drinker, but she knew she would need a little help to get her through the night and stopped at the store on her way home. Maybe it would help her make the right decision and rid her of the anguish that pained her mind, body, and soul. The voice she heard only a few hours ago was in her head, and according to him, he

NEEDED to see her. Why did she give in and give Felix her address? She missed him terribly—that's why.

Jennifer wondered how she could continue to convince her bleeding heart and her sexually starved body that Felix was not the man she needed. She closed her eyes and recalled their time together. Never had a man captured her heart and her body in such a manner. She was head over heels in love, and she knew it. But Felix, as wonderful as he was, was also very married. He claimed he was in a marriage of convenience so he could wake up in the same home as his only son every day. He told Jennifer he and his wife no longer shared the same bed, and it had been over a year since they coupled as husband and wife. Jennifer didn't understand how any woman in her right man could deny that divine specimen of manhood entrance into her sacred place. She believed everything Felix told her. He pretended to lay it all on the table—every wound, every battle scar he obtained while in a loveless marriage and asked her to somehow make it better. He looked so dejected as he confided his unhappiness. Jennifer made it her mission to soothe every hurt with her own special love-laced body balm, taking Felix's pain away, but in the process, inflicting it on herself. She fought to extract Cupid's arrow from her heart, but it wouldn't budge. She called off their affair multiple times, but somehow, within a few weeks, she always found herself again entangled in his embrace as they declared their love for each other. She knew Felix loved her, but he loved life with his son more. At least that's what he told her. She couldn't compete with an adorable five-year-old, and she wasn't a monster. What kind of woman would take a child's father away? She grew up without one. She wouldn't do that to an innocent little boy.

Jennifer believed Felix to be the victim of a loveless union . . . until one day she saw him and his family in a restaurant, and for over an hour she willingly tortured herself by watching him kiss, fondle, and hug the woman he claimed he no longer wanted or loved. Their interactions exuded love. He had been lying to her for the past year, and she knew it. She had no one to blame but herself. She knew he was married when she met him. He wore his wedding band every day. After their first encounter, she should have cut him off, but she continued to selfishly date another woman's husband. He made her feel alive and sexy and Jennifer often found herself setting aside her morals and inhibitions and doing things she never thought she'd do, like date a married man. She wasn't without a conscience. She felt like the biggest harlot in Nashville when she spent a sinful week in the Bahamas with him. Yet, she had to admit to herself how nice it was to have him all to herself and wake up beside him every morning. For a few days, she pretended that she was Mrs. Felix Payne, and their time bathing in the beauty of the islands was their honeymoon. But like all honeymoons, it had to end. She was quickly reminded that she was not the Mrs. after their return, and she found herself waking up each morning alone . . . AGAIN. Why did she care so much? If he didn't respect his marriage, why should she? It was because bedding another woman's husband was wrong and she knew it.

All these things ran through Jennifer's head as the voice of her song of choice rang out again with the last few words of the pained song. *Tell me, is it a criiiiiiiiiiime?*

"It sure is. All cheaters deserved to be locked up and starved to death," Jennifer said quietly to herself. She was a fool, but hadn't everyone been a fool for love at some point in their lives?

Felix's voice alone sent shivers down her spine. She almost exploded early today when he uttered the words, "I miss you. I can't breathe without you," on the other end of the phone.

Jennifer told herself that she didn't need him. He was breathing just fine, or otherwise, he'd be dead. Maybe he had developed a case of asthma. She was lonely, bored, and in need of some sexual healing, but she had done well in her refusal to call him. Each time she got the urge to reach out to Felix, she reminded herself that dating him was futile. Her romantic trysts with him seemed to lead to one heartbreaking disappointment after another. This time, she timed her breakup to coincide with her beginning a new job and moving to a new place. This would prevent him from showing up at her job or on her doorstep with flowers, candy, lies, and mind-blowing sex. Her former neighbor called and told her that Felix came over banging on the door so many times she finally went next door and informed him that Jennifer had moved and the house was completely empty. Jennifer even changed her number, but somehow, he got her new one and was once again trying to reinsert himself into her life and her bed.

Everyone has a vice. Some people use drugs, some drink alcohol, others smoke cigarettes; Jennifer's was love. She didn't feel complete if there wasn't someone claiming he loved her. All too often, "I love you" led to a deceitful one-act play that she was oblivious to having a starring role in. Lies were laced with kisses, deadly venom was disguised in the wine served during intimate dinners, soft caresses and lithe licks accompanied orgasmic evenings, and undelivered promises were made right before the final scene when the undeserving hero told her, the heroine, he "didn't want anything serious," "it just wasn't working out," or "I already have someone." Those men were unpaid actors, for sure. Ones worthy of Oscars and Academy Awards.

Jennifer recognized she couldn't blame anyone but herself for this predicament and all the others. There were always signs that she ignored. This time, she was determined to rewrite the scene and change the script to include a happier ending. If she was a vindictive woman, it would have been easy to call his wife and tell her everything and wait to see if the chips fell in her favor. The wife had to know. On more than one occasion, Felix didn't come home until the wee hours of the morning because he was with her. She saw the phone calls that showed up in his phone as Mrs. Payne that went unanswered. Sometimes there was as many as five back-to-back. His wife had to know, but as long as she kept her big house in the wealthy suburbs of Nashville, her luxury car, her unlimited spending account, evidently she didn't care. Felix once confided in her that he didn't have a prenup, and if they ever divorced, she would get a large portion of his current and future earnings. He was a neurosurgeon and earned quite a bit.

A tear rolled from Jennifer's eyes. She was in love in the worst way, but no matter how hard she loved or how much she gave of herself, Felix would eventually go home to another woman. She deserved someone who would give her an expensive, spacious house. She deserved to wear the finest clothes and drive the finest cars. But most of all, she deserved someone who could love her openly and honestly. Someone who wouldn't tell her they can't go to certain restaurants and stores because his family, wife, or coworkers frequented there. She was settling for a mere piece of the pie when she deserved the entire yummy, gooey, delectable thing. There was just one small problem. Jennifer wanted this utopia with Felix. She wanted to be there when he got home from work with dinner on the table wearing nothing but an apron. She knew he would devour her first and come back hours later and heat up his dinner. That's the life she yearned for. She closed her eyes, and the serenity prayer came softly through her wine-tinged lips.

Father, grant me the serenity to accept the things I cannot change, the courage to change the things I can, and the wisdom to know the difference. Amen.

There was a knock at her door. She knew who it was and decided that she wasn't going to answer. She grabbed her bottle of Moscato and quietly retreated up the stairs to her bedroom where she took off her clothes. The knocks grew harder, but she ignored them. Jennifer took one last, long swig, emptying the contents of the bottle and then sat it down on the carpeted floor. She buried herself among the warm, thick folds of her comforter then lay her head on her pillow and fell into one of the most peaceful slumbers she had encountered in a very long time.

Felix was going to learn today that it truly was over. She had to do the right thing for herself and the single man who was going to come into her life and love her the way she deserved to be loved.

The Ex-Files

As a dog returns to its vomit, so fools repeat their folly.
— Proverbs 26:11

"Excuse me. May I borrow a pencil?"

That one question ignited a love affair that I will treasure for the rest of my life. I remember it like it was yesterday. I was in the library, sitting at the information desk and looking down at my precalculus book, trying to figure out the square root of x when I heard it. I raised my head to find myself gazing into one of the handsomest faces I had ever seen, and it belonged to Ryan Willis. He was a dark-skinned dream! I swear that boy was the color of midnight, and his body contained enough muscles to build another man. His chiseled chest and six-pack abs had girls spending their afternoons sweating in the hot sun to see him with his shirt off during football practice. I had seen him around campus several times but never had the courage to speak to him. I never had a reason to. Until then.

"Uh . . . yeah," I said and handed him the one I was using. I really didn't have another pencil but looking into those hazel eyes, Ryan could have asked for my left kidney, and I would have torn a hole in my pelvis with my bare hands and handed it to him on a silver platter.

"Great. I promise I'll bring it back when I'm finished," he said and smiled. As he took the pencil, Ryan's hand gently touched mine, and I swear that I heard violins accompanied by exploding fireworks, and my heart started beating a mile a minute. It was love at first sight. At least, that's what it felt like for me. I think he was like, "She's kind of cute."

Ryan was the kind of man fantasies consisted of. I, on the other hand, was 100 percent nerd. My best attribute was my brain, not my beauty. It was rare that anyone who wasn't on the debate team or chess club even looked at me unless he needed the answer to a test question, or in this case, a pencil.

Ryan took my pencil and headed back over to the jocks study table where they sat with their tutors. The university couldn't have their star players becoming ineligible because of grades, so they made sure that they were equipped to pass their classes. When he brought my pencil back, he told me he was heading over to the cafeteria before they closed for the day and invited me to come. I jumped at the chance. I even left the library information desk unattended. I worked there as a requirement for my scholarship and could have gotten in so much trouble if my supervisor found out I left, but it was a chance I was willing to take. Ryan Willis asked me to have dinner with him! That was evidence that God was still in the blessing business. I was not about to pass up on a blessing.

We walked to the cafeteria, he ordered a chef salad, and I had pizza. That was the best pizza I ever tasted. I still remember that it was a pepperoni with onions and peppers. We ate and talked and even after we finished eating, we just sat and talked some more. Ryan was definitely not a dumb jock. We talked about school, movies, music, politics, racism, and a bunch of other topics I can't remember. It was hard for me to focus while staring into his handsome face, but I managed. I wasn't about to ruin this moment by acting like some spaced-out jock groupie. Ryan and I stayed so late that the cafeteria staff cleaned up around us and then politely asked us to leave when it was time for them to lock up. He asked for my number, but I never expected to hear from him again. I figured that night was too good to be true. He had some of the most beautiful girls on campus after him. Why would he waste time on me?

I was wrong. The next day Ryan called me after practice, and we talked until the wee hours of the morning. That weekend he asked me out on a date. I guess you could call it a date. We went to watch a movie at one of his friends' houses who always had bootlegs of the latest releases. His girlfriend was there, and the guy's parents were nice enough to grill us some burgers. After watching the movie, we all sat on the patio and talked and laughed for hours. Afterward, when Ryan took me back to my dorm, we kissed. This time I didn't just hear violins but an entire symphony, and the explosions were replaced by massive butterflies taking flight! The following days, we hung out on campus in between classes and before and after his practices, and pretty soon, we were a couple. He was my first love. We didn't have sex, though. He said he respected my virginity and my desire to remain chaste until marriage. It wasn't easy for us to remain abstinent, but I'm proud to say we did it. I was head over heels crazy about that man. I would do almost anything for him. Sometimes, I think I did a little too much. I wrote several of Ryan's papers for him and even took the LSAT for him. We could have both been kicked out of school if we'd been caught. I know I shouldn't have, but I wanted him to do well, and sometimes between his regular assignments, practice, and games, Ryan got behind. As his girlfriend, I felt it was my duty to help him catch up. We dated our entire senior year. Graduation was a happy time, but a sad one as well. I had been accepted to grad school at NYU, and he was headed off to Southern University for law school. We were both smart enough to know that our relationship could not survive the distance. We were broke students. Who was going to pay for the flights?

I hated to leave him, but I knew I had to. If it was meant to be, we'd find each other again. I was sure of it. I can't tell you how many nights I cried myself to sleep because the pain of missing him was so great. I had my rigorous NYU studies to thank for helping me get through it. Then there was Aaron, my ex-husband. He was most definitely a pleasant distraction from any lingering memories of Ryan I may have had. Once again, I fell head over heels for a man, but this one asked me to be his lawfully wedded wife. I was married at 24, and divorced by 28. I don't think either of us was ready for marriage, but we were so in love. We couldn't imagine one without the other, but once we began living under the same roof, our incompatibilities became too much. We realized that we really didn't know each other, and we didn't have much in common. We were always fighting and two weeks before our third anniversary, Aaron moved out and filed for divorce.

After my divorce, I heard, through mutual friends, that Ryan had dropped out of law school and was working as a coach in Greenville, Mississippi for some program for disadvantaged youth. That didn't surprise me because Ryan had always been good with kids. In college, we volunteered at the local YMCA sometimes, and he was always leading them in some kind of physical activity and encouraging them to do well in school. He would have the biggest smile on his face, like he loved every minute of it. I still thought about him from time to time, but I didn't try to contact him. There really was no need. We had both moved on. I was a successful human resources professional, and he was wherever, doing whatever. It was a beautiful college romance, but it was very much over.

Next week is my 30th birthday, and I recently moved to Cincinnati after accepting a position as the head of HR with a major IT company. My new job is challenging, but I enjoy it, and I love Cincinnati. It's a nice medium between the Southern life in Mississippi, where I grew up, and the bright lights, fast pace, and expensive cost of New York. I haven't started dating anyone yet, but my job is so demanding, it's hard to find time to go out. After work, all I want to do is go home and get some sleep. If I had a boyfriend, his name would be Pillow or Serta because sleep is the only thing I do in my free time.

I was more than a little surprised when, one day, my administrative assistant left me a note that Ryan called. I planned to return the call later that evening when I got home from work. I shared my "great news" when my best friend and former college roommate Mariah called to check on me. She was less than thrilled. She never really did like Ryan, though. She swore he only used me for my brains. She was always trying to tell me about some girl she saw him with, but I wouldn't listen. I knew my man wouldn't cheat on me. She was just jealous. Her man lived in another area code, and she only saw him when she went home for the holidays.

"Girl, I heard he wasn't doing too good," said Mariah. "He has at least three kids by three different women, and he works at a gas station. I heard he might even be gay. Trust me, Keitha, you dodged a bullet with that one," she said.

"Ryan . . . gay? Girl, you're trippin'. He loved women. There's no way he's gay."

"I'm just telling you what I heard from Stacey, whose cousin Jacob went to school with us, and he said he saw Ryan coming out of some bar that's popular with the gay locals with his arm draped around some man's waist. When he saw Jacob staring at him, he tried to slide his hand from around the dude."

I laughed. "Jacob with the lazy eye?"

"Yep. That's him."

"That boy was always looking in two directions at the same time. It probably wasn't even Ryan he saw."

Mariah tried to act offended. "For your information, he had corrective surgery on that eye and you are going to hell if you don't stop talking about the visually impaired."

"I never said he couldn't see. I said he couldn't see *straight*. Thanks for the heads-up, but I think I'll take my chances. What harm could it be to catch up with an old friend? It's just a phone call."

"Suit yourself, but I say an ex is an ex for a reason, and the past has no reason to be invited into your present."

"Duly noted. Bye, Mariah."

"Bye, Keitha. Don't you let that man ask you to write a paper or take a test for him."

Leave it to Mariah to make me laugh while making me feel foolish. "Shut up," I said and hung the phone up in her face.

I returned Ryan's call that evening, and it was really nice to hear his voice. He said he looked me up online because he planned to be in town the following week and wanted to know if he could see me. I didn't see a problem with that. I thought my birthday was going to be boring since I didn't have any friends in the area yet, but I might have a happy birthday after all. He started asking me about hotels in the area. I told him not only could he see me but he could save the hotel money and crash at my place.

On the day of his arrival, I left work early and prepared a wonderful home cooked meal. I had baked salmon with rice pilaf and sautéed spinach. If he was still the same Ryan I remembered, he would love it because he was a pretty healthy eater. We could have gone out, but I wanted to be able to talk to him without the distraction of other people. We hadn't really talked in almost six years. I figured afterward we could go out for dessert.

When I opened the door, I thought the cousin of the angel Gabriel was standing on my doorstep. Ryan had this beckoning ethereal glow around him, and I wanted to take him in my arms and smother him in kisses. He looked better than he did in college. He was a boy then, but standing in front of me was a fully mature man. He had a few extra pounds here and there, but that was to be expected. It was obvious he still worked out regularly. I had gained a few pounds myself, but they were all in the right places. I had been trying to practice abstinence for the last year for religious reasons, but I didn't know if I was going to make it through this weekend. I would let fate decide. If it happened, it happened, but I wouldn't be the one to prevent it from happening. I'd try hard not to initiate it.

I knew Ryan had to be famished from his drive from Mississippi, so I showed him to my spare room and told him to wash up for dinner. We had a pleasant conversation during our meal. We talked about old times and new times. He told me that he couldn't afford law school, and that's why he had to drop out. He did inform me that he had three children, but they were all by the same woman. He met her while he was coaching football at a local junior high. The two of them never married, though. He was currently working as a substitute teacher and at an afterschool program for children with behavioral problems. He liked working with children, but he couldn't teach because he wasn't certified. It didn't sound like he made much money, but it was rewarding work.

Ryan raved about how good the food was, and the man ate like he hadn't eaten in years. When he picked up the plate and licked the last bit of juice from the salmon and spinach, all I could do was laugh and shake my head. Somebody needed to teach him some dining etiquette. However, I must admit the way he licked that plate *did* turn me on. After dinner, I told him to get dressed because I was taking him out. I went to the bathroom to freshen up a little bit when I heard my phone chime. I checked to see who it was, and it was Ryan.

WE DON'T HAVE TO GO OUT TONIGHT. I'M TOTALLY OKAY IF YOU WANT TO STAY IN.

Why was he texting me, and we're in the same house? It sounded like someone wanted to start the birthday celebration early, but I wasn't going out like that. He was going to have to work a little bit harder to get this pudding cup. I prepared dinner; the least he could do was take a sister out for dessert. I waited until I was done getting ready to give him a reply.

I walked out wearing the tightest dress I owned. His gorgeous hazel eyes widened when I made my entrance, but he didn't say anything. It was obvious he liked what he saw, and I was expecting some sort of compliment but didn't get one. "Why in the world would you want to come to a city you've never been to and stay in? You're only here for one night. No, sir, we're going out. Get your jacket," I said. Ryan followed directions and got his jacket.

I took him to The Cheesecake Factory. We ate dessert and gazed into each other's eyes. It was nice being close to him again. It felt right, like it was meant to be. After a couple of hours, I was perfectly okay with returning to my house for some adult fun time. I hinted that I was ready to go, and Ryan waved the server over. I noticed that he hesitated and looked at me before giving him his debit card, but I didn't think much of it because surely he didn't expect me to pay.

The server returned a few minutes later and said, "Sir, your card was declined."

"I thought this might happen. K, baby, can you get this? I used my teacher's credit union card, and I don't think it works outside of the state."

Did he *really* just say that? I shot him a dirty look and pulled out my credit card. Who goes out of town with no money? My mother always taught me that broke people should stay home. I decided not to let that ruin our evening, though. It was only twenty-two bucks. I suggested we take a short stroll before we headed to the car. It was nice outside. The temperature was in the low 80's, and a slight breeze made it absolutely perfect. There was a full moon above that set the perfect mood for a romantic reconnection of two lovebirds who had been away from each other for way too long. I bought some sexy lingerie that I knew he was going to love because it was his favorite color, blue. I was ready to put it to good use. I looped my small arm around his strong, massive one and squeezed. It was all muscle. That moment reminded me of when we used to take late-night strolls across campus. The stars were twinkling in the sky, and it was as if the moon was our own personal spotlight. It was just me and my first love, and it felt like everything was as it should be.

"You look really good tonight, K," said Ryan. I had finally gotten my compliment. *Yes!* "You didn't have all that booty in college."

I laughed. "Yeah, it seems like getting older agrees me. Thank you. You look really good too. I was surprised to hear from you after all this time. I thought you had forgotten about me. I'm glad you called."

"Me, forget about you? You never forget your first love."

"I guess you're right," I said in my best seductive voice. I pushed my face closer to his, closed my eyes and waited for him to kiss me. I knew it was going to be as magical as it was all those years ago on campus. Nothing happened. I opened my eyes to find Ryan looking in another direction like he didn't realized that I wanted a kiss. That was awkward. I suggested we make our way back to the car.

"Good idea," he said.

We made insignificant small talk during the drive. Once we returned to my place, I checked to see if he had plenty of towels in the guest bathroom and retired to my room. The night hadn't gone like I hoped, but he would be there tomorrow. Maybe he wanted to take things slow. I lay down on my king-sized bed and turned on the TV. After flipping through several channels, I determined that nothing good was on. I heard a soft knock at my door, and Ryan pushed his handsome head in.

"You asleep?"

"Nope. Come on in." I scooted over in the bed and motioned for him to join me. Instead of sitting on the bed next to me, he sat down in the armchair close by.

"There's something I should tell you, and it's probably best I say it now rather than later." He took a deep breath before continuing. "I'm engaged."

"What? Then why are you here in my house with me? I know your fiancée didn't tell you it was okay to come spend time with your ex."

"Not exactly, but there's more. I'm engaged to a man."

I wanted to scream, but I didn't. I was trained to remain calm during intense situations. I simply said, "Ryan, help me understand why you are here."

"To be honest, I have a job interview tomorrow, and I didn't have enough money for a hotel. Things have been rough for me lately. I have three kids and their child support takes a huge chunk out of my check. I don't make much. If I don't pay it, my baby momma has no problem putting my behind in jail."

My heart dropped. After all these years, he was *still* using me, and I was *still* his willing fool. BBD said never trust a big butt and a smile in their song "Poison." I needed to write a remix that said never trust a six-pack and a smile. "You found me so you could have a free room and meals during your trip? That's low, Ryan."

"Not exactly. Keitha, I wanted to see you. People have told me several times how good you're doing, and I wanted to see for myself. I mean, I still care about you. Look at this huge house. It's obvious that you are doing it, and doing it well. I want to be just like you when I grow up." He laughed, but I failed to see any humor in the situation.

"But seriously, I've been working nothing but dead-end jobs for five years. I can't seem to catch a break. I even applied to be a sanitation worker, and they told me I was overqualified because I have a degree. My fiancé put me out last week after I didn't have enough money to cover the utilities. He told me that I lacked ambition, and he had serious doubts about my ability to take care of him. If I can land this job, I'd show him that I do, and maybe he'll take me back. I'd be making more than him, so I know he would have no problem moving out here with me. Please don't be mad at me, but I was afraid if I told you the truth you wouldn't let me stay."

Was God punishing me for wanting to get my freak on? My ex-boyfriend is sitting here in my home telling me about how he was trying to provide for another dude. Did I look like Dr. Phil, Oprah, or Iyanla? This was too much!

"Ryan, look at me. Do I look like I just wanted to talk tonight? I was hoping to get laid."

His eyes traveled from my face all the way down to my feet. "How was I supposed to know that after all these years you would still be attracted to me? I figured you would have had plenty of men since me. College was a long time ago. We didn't even have sex."

How could I have been so stupid? I should have put him out right then, but I needed answers. "How long have you known you were gay?"

"I was always slightly attracted to men, but I was much more attracted to women. At first it was just a desire to be in the company of attractive men. So I would make them my friends. Being around them seemed to be enough. I never wanted to kiss them or anything like that. I enjoyed their company and looking at them, I guess."

I thought back to college. All of Ryan's friends were fine, and most of them were athletes. The girls on campus used to call them The Bomb Squad and The Moist Makers. He always had five or six guys with him that were every bit as sexy and handsome as him or more. Girls would flock to them wherever they were.

"When I was in law school I had a roommate who was openly gay but still very masculine, and he was attracted to masculine-looking men. One night, I shared with him what I was feeling, and when I woke up the next morning, he was in my bed. I started to protest, but he said, 'Just go with it and see if you like it.' He laid in bed with me talking and cuddling for hours, and it didn't feel weird or wrong. We did small things like that, and then one day, he kissed me and things went a lot further."

I didn't need to hear anymore. "You can spare me the details. Sounds like you got turned out," I said.

"I guess you could say that. When I left law school, I tried to fight those feelings. That's how I ended up with the kids, but later, I met a guy I had an amazing connection with and gave in. Baxter is wonderful, and I don't want to lose him."

It was time to change the subject. I had no desire to hear all about Baxter. "What time is your interview?"

"At 3 p.m. I'm really nervous."

"Get up. Show me what you're wearing, and then I'll help you prepare. I know almost every interview tip and trick there is."

"Really? Thank you, K. You're the best. I'll never forget you."

"Oh yes, you will. After you leave don't ever contact me again, and you better not ever tell anyone that you came here to visit me and tried to use my home as a bed and breakfast. Do you understand me?" I had my "I mean business" face on, and I meant every word I said.

"Don't you think you're taking this a bit too far? I mean, we were college sweethearts. Can't we remain friends?"

"The key word there is *were*. As you reminded me, college was a long time ago. At least, in college, you were a little more creative when you were broke. You'd tie me up all night kissing on me so we would stay in."

"You knew?"

"Of course, I knew that's what you were trying to do. But why would I complain about you being affectionate? I liked having you all to myself anyway. Whenever we went out, it seemed like your friends always found us. I didn't want to hang with those people anyway. The only reason all the popular students were even nice to me was because I was dating you. Now, get out of my room."

Ryan didn't budge. "You know, people used to ask me what I saw in you. I always told them you had a great personality and an amazing heart, and if they took the time to get to know you, they'd see it too. I always thought you were cute in an intelligent Velma on *Scooby-*

Doo kind of way. I may have changed, but I'm happy to see that you haven't. You've still got an amazing heart. You've also blossomed into a gorgeous woman."

That was sweet but all wasn't forgiven. "Yeah, whatever. You and my education were the only good things that came from me attending that school. And I said get out of my room."

Ryan left to lay his clothes out. I told him I would be there shortly to check out what he had. I needed a minute to myself. I was hurt, disappointed, and a little mad. I wanted to tell him to leave, but I knew he had no place to go. He'd probably sleep in his car all night. Our history wouldn't let me treat him like that. I was a nerdy nobody until he noticed me in the library. In a matter of weeks, my position on campus shot up to dime status. His friend's girlfriends gave me a makeover. They showed me how to pick out clothes that were trendy and complemented my body type. They helped me do my hair and makeup. I knew it was so I wouldn't embarrass them when we all hung out together, but I didn't care. It was nice being popular, but there was one perk I enjoyed the most. Ryan treated me like a queen, and he boosted my confidence to a place it had never been before. He told me I was pretty when I thought I wasn't. I never thought I could have a man like him, let alone get him to fall in love with me. He showed me what the love of a good man could do for a woman, and for that, I would be eternally grateful. Girls were all in his face when I wasn't around, but I wasn't worried. He told me repeatedly that I was the only woman for him. He also never let anyone disrespect me in his presence. When people tried to make snide remarks about us being together or other girls tried to flirt with him, he made sure they knew that would not be tolerated. I wouldn't have applied to NYU if it wasn't for him. In my small-mindedness, I didn't see what a country girl like me was going to do in the big city. It was Ryan who told me that I could do anything and go anywhere if I put my mind to it. He even downloaded the application and brought it to me to complete. I was going to do this for him to say thank you. Afterward, I never wanted to see him again.

As I got up and walked down the hallway, the words of Mariah came back to me. "You dodged a bullet with that one." I had to admit that she was right. Baxter could have him.

Ryan didn't know one thing about dressing to impress, but he had worn sweat suits and basketball shorts most of his life. I helped him coordinate his suit, shirt, and shoes. I even gave him a pair of unisex trouser socks I picked up recently that really set off the shirt he was wearing. Since the interview was for a midlevel position with a sports management company, I decided he could forgo the tie. I even ironed and starched his shirt and shined his shoes before I went to bed.

The next morning, I called in to work to take the day off. After he cooked breakfast, I coached Ryan on how to behave and the proper way to answer interview questions. We practiced all morning. By noon, we were both confident that he was prepared to present himself as an impressive candidate for the position. Ryan got dressed, and I gave him a good look from head to toe. I had to admit that he cleaned up nicely. If the interviewer was a woman, he had nothing to worry about. He looked impressive in his navy suit with his Periwinkle shirt. He loaded his things up in his car before he left for the interview. I made it clear that he would not be returning to my home. EVER.

He seemed kind of sad as he said his good-bye, but I didn't care. I didn't need a gay, manipulative, ex-boyfriend in my life. "I'm really sorry we have to part like this. I apologize for not being honest about my intentions. I wish you would reconsider," he said.

My mind was made up. "No, after the stunt you pulled, I'd prefer to keep my distance. Good luck on your interview. Do what I told you and you should be fine. I wish you a glorious future, but I want no part of it," I said.

He leaned over and kissed me on the cheek. "There's a guy somewhere looking for a good woman like you."

"Sure. If you meet him, give him my address. Maybe he'll find me if he doesn't fall in love with a man first. Now, go knock'em dead, Romeo."

He smiled at hearing the nickname I gave him in college. "That's cold, K," said Ryan before exiting my home and my life for good. After he left, I took a nap. He hadn't been in town a full 24 hours, and I was emotionally drained. I decided not to tell anyone what happened, not even Mariah. Some things were better left between you, the other person, and the four walls.

A couple of days later while sitting at my desk at work, I got a text from Ryan.

I GOT CALLED BACK FOR A SECOND INTERVIEW. THANK YOU SO MUCH. DO YOU MIND IF I CRASH AT YOUR PLACE AGAIN? ☺

I sent him a picture of a middle finger. I'm sure he got the point.

Just Have Faith

Therefore I tell you, whatever you ask for in prayer, believe that you have received it, and it will be yours. — Mark 11:24

I completed my stretches and started slowly down the trail surrounding my apartment complex. I gained a steady pace and looked up toward the heavens. It was a warm and clear day. The sky was so blue and beautiful. The sun shined brightly on my worried face. I always believed that such beauty was outward evidence that there was a God, He was truly amazing, and today I needed Him in the worst way. I felt the rise and fall of my breasts as I trotted along. I breathed in deeply and could almost taste the nearby forest. I loved the smell of pine needles. The back of my apartment complex was surrounded by a wooded area, and my run next to the trees was always a welcomed activity. There was just something about nature. It was one of the things that man couldn't create but was always trying to control.

I ran so often I could almost run the trail with my eyes closed. I probably would have if it wasn't for the possibility that I might bump into another runner. It didn't matter the season or the temperature. Since I discovered track in middle school, I'd always felt the need to run. It somehow gave my life balance. At least, it used to. The scene from two days ago invaded my thoughts and interrupted what little peace I had. I kept hoping, wishing, and praying that it was a dream, and I would wake up at any moment. That dreadful conversation would not stop echoing in my head.

"Congratulations, Ms. Austin. You are pregnant," said Dr. Ferguson.

I immediately dropped my head and covered my face with my hands. The tears stung as they emerged from my eyes. That was not what I wanted to hear.

"I assume this isn't a good thing," she said.

"It's a horrible thing," I choked out.

Dr. Ferguson took my hand in hers, patted it gently, and spoke softly. "I believe that babies are a blessing from God, but if you feel that strongly about it, there are other options. I'll give you some literature to take home. Why don't you take a few days to think about it? Parenthood can be a joyous journey, but should look forward to the trip. Everything is going to be all right, young lady."

I wished I believed her. I messed up big time. I can't believe this is happening to me. How did I get so sloppy? Our last time was supposed to be the last time, but now it seems like it's only the beginning. Six weeks ago, I went to Nate's place to finally end our relationship, and instead of saying my piece and then leaving, I gave into my carnal desires. We still broke up, but why didn't I leave as I planned? That man always did know how to have his way with me. I hadn't talked to him since. I couldn't even pick up the phone to tell him about the pregnancy. I went by his job but couldn't bring myself to go in, so I left a note on his car instead. I want kids, but not now, and not this way. Baby mama wasn't a title I aspired to hold. CEO, president, director of such-and-such . . . Those are titles I can get down with. *I'm supposed to be going to Spain this summer for an internship. I can't go four months pregnant. How am I going to tell my parents? My life is over. I had such a promising future. Maybe I should make this problem simply disappear. Then all will be fine. No one will ever know, except Nate. I could lie and tell him I was kidding.* As all those thoughts raced through my head, I ran faster and faster. It was if I was trying to outrun my situation, but I knew within my heart, my problem would be right there growing within my stomach. No matter how fast I run, I can't run from myself, or better yet, from what is inside of me. I stopped. I was hot, tired, and panting uncontrollably.

"Hello, Ashley," I heard a familiar voice say. "I thought I would find you back here."

"What are you doing here?" I said in between deep breaths.

"You won't answer any of my calls. I went by your job, and they told me you called in sick today. So I figured I'd come over," Nate said.

"You should have called or sent a text or something."

"So you could leave before I got here? No way. Now, is that any way to talk to the father of your child?"

Nate stepped forward and caressed my face with one hand. "You always looked radiant to me after a run. Your face is all rosy. You are one of the most beautiful creatures I've ever laid eyes on."

I backed away. "Don't touch me. That's what got us here! Your relentless need to touch me. Is there something I can do for you?"

"Actually, there is. Can we go inside and talk?"

He looked so earnest and sincere, but I had to stand strong. No amount of sweet talk was going to improve this situation. "No. Whatever you need to say, you need to say it now, and then leave," I said sternly.

"Okay." Nate pulled something out of his pocket and then got down on one knee. "Ashley Leigh Austin, will you do me the honor of being my wife and the mother of our amazing child?" he said.

I think my heart stopped—or at least skipped a beat. For a moment, I could have sworn that everything halted. The earth and I were at a complete standstill. I gave Nate a sidelong glance. *What was he doing?* He was a small man compared to most. He was 5'11" and about 200 pounds, but it was mostly muscle. He worked out every day before or after work. He was handsome, and I was captivated by his eyebrows. They were thick and ebony and served as the perfect adornment for his wide, brown eyes. They looked like two pools of luscious milk chocolate, and I was smitten from the moment he said,

"Hello, miss, how can I help you?" when I walked into the auto repair shop where he worked.

I needed an oil change. He was working the counter that day and was dressed in a suit, so I thought he might be the owner's son. We had a nice conversation as I waited for them to finish my car. When he asked me out, I thought, why not? Later that week, he took me to Red Lobster. I love Red Lobster. Their cheddar biscuits are to die for, and that raspberry tea always hits the spot. I was captivated by him. The way he told a story made you hang on to every word until he was finished. During our date, I found out he was a student, like me, and only worked part-time at the shop. The reason he had on a suit that day was because he was returning to work after attending a funeral, but I didn't care that he wasn't the owner's son. He had ambition and goals. I wanted to see him again, and see him I did. Anytime that I could. He might as well have moved into my apartment because when I wasn't in class, studying, or at my part-time job, I was with him.

He didn't care that I was celibate and never pressured me for anything. He told me anything worth having was worth waiting for. I had no intentions of sleeping with him, or anyone else, for that matter. It had been hammered into my head since I was a little child to be a woman of virtue and grace. Only "common women" gave away their essence of womanhood to anyone other than their husband, and the daughter of Pastor Obadiah Austin of Houston, TX was anything but common.

About three months into our courtship, we had a terrible snowstorm, and the roads were way too treacherous for him to drive home. Nate spent the night. He made a cozy little fire in my electric fireplace, and while we sat in front of it listening to Luther Vandross, he recited a poem he wrote about me that beautifully illustrated how much he loved me. I had never heard anything so touching in my life. At the end of the poem, he kissed me, and I didn't want him to stop. We had kissed passionately before, and sometimes I would allow his hands to roam a little. I enjoyed the feel of his hands against my skin. He worked with them daily, but they were amazingly soft. Yet, this time when he reached underneath my shirt and began to caress my body, I didn't tell him to stop. I wanted him to continue. I yearned for him to continue. I needed him to put into deed everything he shared with me poetically. I wanted to feel how he felt about me, as well as hear it. I'd heard the girls in my classes say their first time wasn't all that. I can't express those same sentiments. My first time was beautiful, and afterward, I was like a dope fiend, and he was my fix. However, after a couple of months, I began to feel convicted, and I wanted to stop. That's when our problems began. Nate told me that you can't lead a thirsty man to a well, let him drink his fill, and then when he's thirsty again, tell him there is no more when he can clearly look into the well and see there's plenty of water left. Sexual desire wasn't a light switch a man could just cut on and off. But I couldn't keep doing what we were doing and feel good about our relationship. Actually, I felt downright tragic about it. So, to maintain my relationship with my God, I broke up with my man. These six weeks without him have been torture. When I started to feel nauseated and my breasts began to ache, I thought my psychological and emotional condition had manifested itself into a physical condition, that's all. Now, on top of being pregnant, he was proposing to me. Why was he doing this? We weren't even together.

"What? We broke up," I said.

"That wasn't my decision. It was yours. I was wondering how I was going to get you back. Now we have the answer. Be my wife. I'm miserable without you. I'm not willing to lose you, Ashley. God told me to do this."

"He did? When did you and God get so cool? I could barely get you to say grace, and now y'all passing notes." I pulled my hoody closer as a small but cool breeze blew in our direction.

"Stop with the sarcasm, Ashley. He told me through a dream. You and I were at the altar and your father was officiating. Your sister was your maid of honor, and your mother was your matron of honor."

I shuddered from the chill. "You're cold, come here." Nate stepped forward and pulled me into him. He wrapped his arms around me, but I didn't do the same. I leaned in to put my head on his chest, but thought better of it and jerked away.

"No, you did that on purpose. You had unprotected sex with me the night I broke up with you, hoping you would get me pregnant. How could you? You know I have big plans for my future!"

Nate looked at me with hurt in his eyes. "No, I did not. I had sex with you, hoping to change your mind. I was hoping you would feel what you've always felt when you're with me and realize that you were making a terrible mistake. Why is making love to the one you love such a horrible thing? You always said God is love, so I can't believe that He would create such a beautiful act between two people and then condemn us to hell for doing it because we haven't stood in front of a preacher. You ended a great relationship because you felt guilty about having sex. What did you call it . . . convicted? There was nothing wrong with us. I understand your dedication to your faith, but what about your dedication to me, to us, our love? I LOVE you. I didn't think I was ready to settle down, but in light of the present circumstances, I am. I want us to be a family. I'm not going to parent my child from another residence. I had a father in the home, and I know how much better my life was because of it. I want to give that to my children."

"I don't want to marry a man who only wants me because I'm pregnant with his baby. I want a man who wants *me!*" I screamed.

Nate looked up to the heavens and threw up both his hands. "Ashley, what is wrong with you? Didn't you hear me say I LOVE YOU? I don't understand you. You broke up with me because you felt guilty about the things we were doing. You said our relationship was unsaved. Now, you are pregnant out of wedlock, and I'm willing to do right by you, and you can't see the good in this because it's not all wrapped up in a pretty bow. Life is not perfect, but we are. Let me love you and this baby. I'm sorry this didn't happen the right way with me asking your father first for your hand in marriage and then getting married and having a baby, but why can't you see the blessing in this? We can still make this right. We can get married and have all the sex we want without you feeling convicted, and raise this wonderful little person that has my DNA and yours. I don't want to see my kid only on the weekends. It's not like we don't love each other. We merely see the world differently."

My heart was slowing melting, but I remained defiant. Nate always knew the right thing to say. What if he was just saying the right thing now and really didn't mean any of it? "Who said I was keeping it?" I said.

"I know better. If you feel guilty about having sex, how much more guilty would you feel about abortion? You're bluffing," said Nate.

Nate lowered himself back down on one knee and grabbed my hand and slid the ring on my finger. This time, I didn't turn away. Tears welled up in my eyes. I really did love this man. No, I didn't feel good about the things we were doing. Well, I didn't feel good afterward. No one had ever made me feel the things he did, but that wasn't how I was raised. I was supposed to wait until I was married. I had disappointed myself and would disappoint my parents once I told them, but most of all, I had disappointed God. What could I do about it now? Nate was right. There was no way I was going to abort my baby. But I needed to know something.

"When I asked if we could return to a celibate relationship, you said there was no way you could be in a relationship without sex after beginning to have sex. Then, when I mentioned marriage, you said you weren't ready for marriage. What changed your mind?"

"You did. I have been absolutely miserable without you. I feel like a piece of my heart is MIA. I bought this ring a week ago, Ashley, before either of us knew you were pregnant. I like who I am when I'm with you. You make me better. It's not that I couldn't see myself married to you, but we're both still young and trying to find our place in the world. I don't even make a decent living yet. You're not the only one with dreams, and my dream is to be able to provide a good life for my wife and children. What I've realized while we've been apart is that my place is right beside you . . . protecting you, providing for you, and loving you. My love for you only makes me want to work harder to be able to adequately care for you and our child."

I looked down at the ring he placed on my finger. It was small but beautiful. It glistened brightly in the afternoon sun. I had to admit that it looked lovely on my finger. A lump was forming in my throat. I knew he meant every word he said. I didn't want to take it off. I wasn't going to take it off.

"Will you marry me? I promise to be a good husband to you. You can still pursue the doctorate degree you want and anything else you want to do. Marry me, Ashley. I don't have all the answers, but what I do know is God brought us together, and right now, the only thing keeping us apart is you."

"But I want a Christian husband. A man who is deeply rooted in Christ. A man who knows how to pray to God and ask Him to cover him and his family," I said.

"I'll probably never be a preacher like your father, but I promise that I'll work on my relationship with God. You're going to have to be patient. I didn't grow up in church like you did. My father didn't see much use for religion, but I see what God has done for you and your family. I even went to church after we broke up. I feel so empty without you. I needed something. While I was there, I prayed for God to fix this."

Nate was still on one knee. I told him to stand up. "I need you to leave. I'm not saying no, but I need you to leave."

"Why? When can I expect an answer?" I could hear the agony in his voice.

"You said God told you to marry me, right?" Nate nodded. "I need you to leave so I can ask Him. You'll get your answer when He gives me mine."

Nate kissed me on my lips. Tears began to stream from my eyes. I loved this man with all my heart, but I had to ask God to lead me in the right direction. I had gone down the wrong path already. I didn't want to keep doing it.

This wasn't how I dreamed my life would be. I was supposed to fall deeply and madly in love with a pastor, deacon, or elder. He was supposed to ask me to be his bride during a romantic dinner at my favorite restaurant with my favorite artist serenading me from a piano. I wasn't supposed to be standing in the back of my apartment complex wearing a track suit and dripping with perspiration, pregnant. My husband-to-be was supposed to be in a suit, not some grimy jumper covered in oil and dirt from the garage where he worked.

"Lord, what's going on here?" I shouted to the sky. I ran home, leaving Nate standing in the back of my apartment complex alone. As soon as I burst through my front door, I fell to my knees and asked God to tell me what to do.

He did, and I was obedient. One month later, Nate and I were standing in my father's church as he officiated our wedding. It wasn't the fairy-tale wedding I had planned in my head since I was a little girl playing with Barbies, but it was nice, nonetheless. Nate looked so handsome in his suit. We had a small, intimate ceremony in the middle of the week. Only our closest friends and family were invited. I married the man I love, and he loves me in return. We are going to share that love with our child. Everyone should be so lucky.

Nate enrolled in a six-month, accelerated, X-ray technician program. After graduating, he should be placed in a new job making a lot more money. He plans to continue to work on cars on his off days. I've never seen him so motivated before. He's determined that he is going to be able to provide for all three of us well. This wasn't the way I envisioned my life, but sometimes, you have to trust God and just have faith.

THANK YOU FOR JOINING ME ON THIS LITERARY JOURNEY!

BE ENCOURAGED!

STAY CONNECTED

Websites

www.jaehendersonauthor.com
www.imagoodwoman.com

Facebook Fan Page
www.facebook.com/imagoodwoman

Twitter
www.twitter.com/jae_henderson

YouTube
www.youtube.com/jaehenderson

Instagram
www.instagram.com/jaehendersonauthor

Blog: My Side of the Single Life
www.mysideofthesinglelife.com

Email
Imagoodwoman2@yahoo.com

Book Clubs
For book club discussion questions visit,
www.jaehendersonauthor.com

If you enjoyed this book, please leave a review on the
Amazon.com, Barnesandnoble.com or Goodreads.com.

www.ingramcontent.com/pod-product-compliance
Lightning Source LLC
Chambersburg PA
CBHW071353170626
46811CB00003B/1120